Celebrate 15 years with

HARLEQUIN®

I N T R I G U E®

Because romance is the ultimate mystery...

The thrill of a secret lover and the excitement of an unknown threat have always been trademarks of Harlequin Intrigue. And thanks to you, our faithful readers, we are here to celebrate 15 years of breathtaking romance and heart-stopping suspense—an irresistible combination.

And we've got plenty to keep you on the edge of your seat in the coming months!

✓ more 43 LIGHT STREET stories by Rebecca York, and Caroline Burnes's FEAR FAMILIAR—your favorite ongoing series!

✓ THE LANDRY BROTHERS—a *new* series from Kelsey Roberts

✓ and THE McCORD FAMILY COUNTDOWN, a special promotion from three of your best-loved Intrigue authors

Intensity that leaves you breathless, romances that simmers with sexual te... them at Harlequin Intrigue

Thank you,

From the Editors

D1059339

ABOUT THE AUTHORS

Ruth Glick writing as Rebecca York

Ruth started her career with newspaper and magazine writing, but her real love was fiction, which she began writing in 1980. In addition to romance and romantic suspense, she has authored eleven cookbooks. She has twice been a RITA finalist for Harlequin Intrigue novels, is the recipient of two Lifetime Achievement awards from *Romantic Times Magazine* and has received the Washington Romance Writers Outstanding Achievement Award. She and her husband make their home in Maryland.

Caroline Burnes

Caroline began writing the Fear Familiar series in 1988. Since that time, Familiar has had ten exciting adventures, and this novella makes eleven. Familiar has covered the United States and traveled to Ireland and Scotland to solve mysteries and work the magic of romance for his adopted "humanoids." Caroline loves all animals and owns one black cat, E. A. Poe, who is the prototype for the demanding Familiar.

AFTER DARK

Rebecca York
Ruth Glick writing as Rebecca York

Caroline Burnes

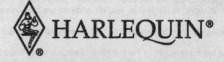

HARLEQUIN®

TORONTO • NEW YORK • LONDON
AMSTERDAM • PARIS • SYDNEY • HAMBURG
STOCKHOLM • ATHENS • TOKYO • MILAN • MADRID
PRAGUE • WARSAW • BUDAPEST • AUCKLAND

ISBN 0-373-22525-3

AFTER DARK

COUNTERFEIT WIFE
Copyright © 1999 by Ruth Glick

FAMILIAR STRANGER
Copyright © 1999 by Carolyn Haines

Visit us at www.romance.net

Printed in U.S.A.

Rebecca York

Ruth Glick writing as Rebecca York

Counterfeit Wife

Previous titles by REBECCA YORK
43 Light Street books:

Peregrine Connection books:

Don't miss the next 43 Light Street:
Midnight Caller
October 1999

Don't miss any of our special offers. Write to us at the
following address for information on our newest releases.

Harlequin Reader Service
U.S.: 3010 Walden Ave., P.O. Box 1325, Buffalo, NY 14269
Canadian: P.O. Box 609, Fort Erie, Ont. L2A 5X3

Prologue

The moon was a bloodred disk hanging in the dark sky. It was big. Scary. Like so many things in the child's young life.

She pulled away from the window and stuck the outside of her index finger into her mouth, sucking to comfort herself as she cringed from the terror waiting to swallow her up.

Big girls weren't supposed to suck their fingers. Mommy would be mad if she saw her doing it. But Mommy wasn't here. She had taken the car and gone...somewhere. With Nick.

She shivered as angry voices drifted to her from downstairs. It was Daddy, Uncle Vance, and the man named Doo Valve with the creepy voice and the mean eyes.

They had all come here to this broken-up house in one of the cars and the van with no windows, driving fast through the black night because Daddy was sick. He had wanted to call someone named Doc Wayne. Uncle Vance had said that was a bad idea.

Suddenly it was quiet. Maybe Doo Valve had taken the station wagon and gone away. The little girl ran down the steps, then tiptoed along the hall to the room where Daddy was lying down.

Uncle Vance was talking, and Daddy was stretched out

on a sleeping bag near the window. In the light from the lantern, she could see blood soaking the bandage on his shoulder.

"Daddy!"

His head jerked toward her. "Lil' Bit," he said, his voice so low she could hardly hear.

Uncle Vance gave her a smile, but she knew he was worried.

"Is everything going to be okay?" she asked, trying to keep her teeth from chattering.

"Yes. Do you want to talk to your daddy?" Uncle Vance asked.

She nodded eagerly.

"Then I'll go find us something to eat."

Slipping into the room, she saw that Daddy's skin looke[d] like paste with beads of water on it.

"Are you gonna die?" she blurted.

"I'm going to be fine."

"Mommy put ant septic on you. It smells bad."

He nodded.

"I'm scared."

"I know, Lil' Bit." His hand reached for her. "Com[e] here so we can talk."

She crept closer till her ear was near Daddy's mouth, s[o] he didn't have to talk loud. Then she heard footsteps behind her. It wasn't Uncle Vance; it was Doo Valve. The bad man.

"What did you tell her?" he growled.

"None of your damn business."

"You're dead wrong." Doo Valve grabbed her daddy by the front of his shirt and shook him, making him groan.

"No!" Rushing at the bad man, she pounded on him with her fists. He whirled, cursed and flung her away. Then everything happened so fast. One minute the lantern was sitting on the floor, the next it was broken on the pile of bandages.

They caught fire, the flames leaping up like bright, hot snakes. Hissing snakes. Doo Valve started beating at them with a blanket. But the blanket caught fire. He threw it down, and the floor began to smoke. Daddy rolled away. With a curse, Doo Valve dived though the window.

Lil' Bit ran toward her father.

"No, get back! Go out the door!" he shouted as the fire licked toward him across the wood floor, making a flaming wall between them.

The room was filling with thick, stinging smoke, and she couldn't see the door, couldn't even see her daddy. Confused, terrified, she spun around, unsure which way to run. The flames roared in her ears. Then she started to cough, her chest burning as she tried to fill her lungs. Flames danced toward her; heat seared her skin. She screamed.

Dimly she heard someone call her name. Then she felt arms grab her, pull her back from the licking orange tongues. There was something wet and cold over her head, and she couldn't see. She could only cling to the strong shoulders of her rescuer as he dragged her from hell.

Chapter One

Heat. Skin-searing heat.

Marianne Leonard hated days like this when the blistering July sun danced on her skin like flames. Slipping into her car, she winced as the seat cover scorched her thighs. Too bad she hadn't found a parking spot in the shade.

Maybe she should move to Alaska, she mused as she gingerly touched the steering wheel. It was worse than the seat, the hard plastic too hot for her fingers to get a good grip.

Lifting her damp golden hair, she leaned toward the vent as the first feeble wisps from the air conditioner stirred the sweltering air. There were a couple of problems with fleeing to the far north: She'd have to give up a great job. And she'd cut herself off from all contact with the Marco family.

Well, not the family, anymore. Mr. Marco had died six months ago. And, to be truthful, she hadn't seen Tony since the reception after the funeral.

She'd spotted him in the corner, isolated from the small crowd of people who had come to pay their respects, his broad shoulders slightly slumped and his chiseled features more daunting than usual. He'd never liked formality, never been comfortable with chitchat. Now he'd taken off his suit jacket and tie—making him stand out in sharp relief to the other men in the room who were still all buttoned up.

The mourners were friends and acquaintances. Not relatives. Like her, Tony was on his own now. Softly, she called his name, and he turned to her with a swiftness that had made her heart leap in her chest. He was tall and solid, yet dark smudges marred the skin under his eyes, and his cheeks had a hollow look that spoke of grief and sleepless nights.

As she crossed the room to stand in front of him, his expression changed, and she saw something flicker in the depths of his dark eyes—something that she'd seen only a few times: Need—basic and primitive—that set off a response deep within her.

"Tony, what can I do?"

At the sound of her voice, his tight expression eased, and he searched her face. "I saw you at the cemetery. You didn't have to drive all the way out there."

"Of course I did. Your dad was like…" She fluttered her hands fumbling for the right words. "He was like a…a kind of stepfather to me."

A warm smile bloomed as memories flooded through her. "He got me through Algebra II. He even taught me to drive. Remember when I stepped on the gas instead of the brake and almost went through the garage door?"

Tony laughed. "He had quite a bit to say about that afterwards."

"The key point is that he didn't bite my head off." She made a small sound of protest. "I'm going to miss him."

Tony nodded solemnly, his total concentration focused on her.

"Let me help," she whispered. "What do you need?"

He didn't answer. But his hand reached toward her in slow motion, and his knuckle stroked across her cheek, then her lips, in a light caress that she felt in all the hidden places of her body.

For several heartbeats, she couldn't move. Then she parted her lips a fraction, giving him the shadow of the kiss that she wanted to press against his mouth, although how she could be having such carnal thoughts at his father's funeral reception was beyond her.

She forgot where they were and why, as his gaze locked with hers, dark and potent. His hand moved to her cheek and then the sensitive line where her jaw met her neck—stroking lightly, sending hot currents through her.

He murmured her name, the barest of whispers. And for a few breath-stopping moments she was sure that his thoughts were running as hot and wild as hers—that he wanted to go someplace where they could be alone and do all the things she had imagined doing with him.

Then his hand fell to his side, and the too-familiar impenetrable mask was once again back in place.

"Tony?"

His shoulders lifted in the barest shrug; then, after a few seconds of stiff conversation, he excused himself and drifted off into the crowd.

The way he'd distanced himself had cut her to the bone. Remembering it still hurt her now—months later.

Unconsciously Marianne tightened her fists around the steering wheel, then loosened her grip as the hot plastic seared her palms.

One by one, she'd lost the people who mattered to her. She supposed her father didn't even count; he'd been out of the picture so long. But her mother had died last year. Then Silvio Marco.

Even before that, for all intents and purposes, she'd lost Tony. Once he'd been like her protective older brother—her defender, her confidant. Then she'd started to mature, and he'd rebuffed her first, shy efforts at changing the relationship. She'd told herself he thought he was too old for her. Maybe that was true when she'd still been a teenager and he was in his early twenties. But the gap had lessened now that they were both adults—for all the good it had done her.

Unconsciously, her lips pressed into a thin line. Really, she should stop obsessing about Tony Marco and try her luck with one of the other guys who wanted to get close to her.

Mom would like that, if she were still alive. Mom had warned her to stay away from him. But Mom hadn't been right about everything.

A flash of movement at the corner of her vision brought her back to the present. With a surge of fear, she swung her head to the side—and saw only a sheet of paper swirling in a sudden updraft.

On a sigh, she ordered her pulse to stop pounding as she pulled out of the parking lot and headed home. For the past few weeks she'd been on edge—seeing things, hearing things, afraid that someone was dogging her steps. Yet each time she whirled to catch sight of her stalker, no one was there.

The irrational anxiety was starting to interfere with her concentration at work—which was darn inconvenient, because as the newest social worker with the Light Street Foundation, she was still trying to prove herself.

Fifteen minutes later, she pulled up beside the kitchen door of the modest bungalow-style house she'd inherited from her mother. It needed fresh paint and a few minor repairs, but basically it was a comfortable place to live—a good place to raise kids, if she ever got married and had any.

Entering through the side door, she set her briefcase on the counter and stood in the middle of the kitchen, thinking that the house smelled wrong. Like stale sweat, she decided. Before she started dinner, she'd better wash the shorts and T-shirt from last night's workout.

She headed for the front door to check the mail, her pocketbook still slung over her shoulder. Halfway across the living room, she stopped. The light in the upstairs hall was on—and she remembered switching it off before coming down.

All the nagging doubts of the past few weeks coalesced

into sudden, choking certainty. Someone had been stalking her, all right. Now he was in the house.

"Little girl, do you remember me?" A soft voice wafted toward her, and she froze. She knew the voice. But it couldn't be. He was dead.

Goose bumps rose on her arms. "Mr. Marco?" she gasped.

The only answer was a laugh—a rich, ghostly laugh that rooted her to the spot where she stood.

"Gotcha!" The voice changed. It was rougher, deeper, mocking.

It wasn't Mr. Marco. Reflexively, she took a quiet step toward the door, then turned and fled. Before she made it across the rug, a hand shot out and grabbed her by the throat, cutting off the scream of terror that rose toward her lips.

Gasping for air, she struggled to wrench herself away, clawing at the hard-as-steel hands that choked off her breath. But the unseen attacker held her fast.

No oxygen reached her lungs, and she felt her vision dim as burly arms dragged her away from the windows. The man was strong, his body rank with sweat.

Black dots danced before her eyes, and she knew she was going to die. Then, just before she passed out, he eased up on the pressure enough for her to gulp in a blessed draft of air.

Keeping his hand clamped on her throat, he lowered himself to the sofa and brought her with him.

Horror was like a wire tightening inside her chest as he held her against his body, her face turned away from him.

"I'm going to take my hand off your windpipe," he growled, his foul breath puffing against her cheek. "If you scream, I'm going to kill you. Nod if you understand."

She managed a small nod, and the hand shifted from her neck to her upper arm. Gasping, she waited to find out what he was going to do, even as she calculated her chances of escape. Next to zero.

She could see his feet encased in black running shoes and his black sweatpants. The sleeve of his T-shirt was also black. It seemed he was dressed for breaking and entering.

Her heart was pounding like a jackhammer inside her chest, but she struggled for calm, trying to take in details.

"I've been waiting a long time for this," he growled.

"For what?" she managed.

"You know damn well."

The words and his confident tone brought a wave of total confusion. "I—I don't know what you're talking about," she croaked, then tried to steady her voice. "And you'd better get out of here because my fiancé is on his way over for dinner."

He laughed again, this time it was a nasty sound that scraped the raw edges of her nerve endings. "Don't play games with me, Miss Marianne Leonard. I've been watching you. I know you don't have any fiancé. You're all alone now that your mom is dead."

"I—"

He cut her off with a snarl, then began to talk in a low, rapid voice that she could hardly follow. He was babbling about her father, saying he had told her a secret. As he spoke, he gave her a shake that rattled her teeth.

Her father? Another ghost from the past. Total mystification fogged her brain. Her father had left their family stranded when she was just a baby—so long ago that she couldn't even remember his face.

"You were there. You know. He told you." The voice in her ear brought her back to the present.

She cringed. "Are—are you sure you have the right woman?"

"No mistake. Even if you did change your name."

"What? My name?"

Meaty fingers dug painfully into her arm. "Don't play games with me. Where is it? Where are you hiding it?"

Marianne tried to keep her brain from going numb, knowing her life might depend on figuring out what this guy was talking about. The only thing she knew for sure was that whatever he wanted she didn't have.

Her mind scrambled, came up with a desperate plan. "You don't think it's here in the house, do you?" she asked in a voice that shook only a little.

"Keep talking!" he growled, and she wondered how she'd ever mistaken his voice for kindly Silvio Marco.

"I...have a letter he left me," she lied, then improvised quickly. "He said not to open it unless I needed his help. It's...it's upstairs. In my room."

He hauled her to her feet, held her as she stood swaying on legs that felt like cooked spaghetti. "One wrong move and I'll shoot you," he warned.

When he gave her a push toward the stairs, she grabbed the lamp table to keep from falling on her face. Did he really have a gun? She hadn't seen it. Maybe he was lying.

She wanted to ask him how he'd get what he wanted if he killed her. She didn't dare confuse him with logic as she stumbled toward the steps, then climbed them slowly, breathing deeply, knowing that she'd better get this right.

A kind of deadly calm descended on her as she reached the upper hall, then took a steadying breath, waiting for him to catch up before she turned right and headed for the spare room.

When she reached the door, she pretended to stumble, her hand going down on the floor as she grabbed for one of the barbells she'd left lying on the exercise mat. Half whirling, she slung the twenty-pound weight at the madman.

It hit him in the stomach, and he gasped, crumpling in surprise as she slammed the door and spared precious seconds to lock it behind her.

Shots sounded, and bullets splintered the wood as she

wrenched open the window and flung herself onto the porch roof.

Too bad he hadn't been lying about the gun.

Using the downspout, she slid to the ground, rounded the house and jumped into the car, her hand fumbling for the keys in the pocketbook that amazingly still dangled from her shoulder.

Angry shouts pursued her to the car. Then the intruder was leaping to the ground like a movie stuntman. In a minute, he'd be on her again.

Her breath coming in ragged gasps, Marianne started the engine, backed out of the driveway, and cannonballed down the block, turning the corner with tires squealing. At the cross street, she turned again, weaving through the familiar neighborhood like a mad dog.

Sparing a quick glance in the rearview mirror, she saw no signs of pursuit—for the moment. Slowing only slightly, she felt between the seats, found her sun hat, and jammed it down over her head. A poor disguise—but it would have to do.

Her first thought was to drive straight to a police station and make a report of the attack. Yet when she actually pictured herself sitting down face-to-face with a detective, she felt a sudden painful tightening inside her chest.

Not the police. She couldn't go to them—because she'd known for as long as she could remember that something about the law had struck a deep, abiding terror in her mom.

A shuddering sigh wracked her chest. Mom was dead. It shouldn't matter. But it did.

There had been so many things she and her mother had never discussed, buried truths simmering below the surface of their seemingly normal existence. And the law was one of those off-limits subjects.

But she'd sensed things, seen things, like the way Mom went rigid when a patrol car pulled up beside them at a red light. And the way her face lost its color when they passed a patrolman at the shopping center.

The police were supposed to be your friends. But Marianne had always known on some deep, subconscious level that they were the enemy. And she'd better stay as far away from them as she could get if she valued her life.

The knowledge brought a kind of terrible despair. She was alone, with no hope of rescue. Then an image of Tony Marco stole into her mind and some of the tightness eased in her chest. Although they had grown apart in the past few years, she still believed he would protect her—the way he had when she'd needed him most. Like when he'd beaten up a gang of boys who were teasing her on the way home from school, saying she didn't have a father. Or when he'd chased off a big black dog that was snapping at her heels.

He would know what to do now, she told herself with a surge of relief. Making a quick right turn at the next intersection, she sped toward the impressive redbrick house he'd bought several years ago. When she pulled up at the curb, however, she saw all the lights were off. And when she rang the bell and pounded on the front door with her fists, there was no answer.

A MILE FROM Marianne Leonard's house, Arlan Duvalle pulled to the curb, his angry curses reverberating in the confines of the stolen car.

He'd thought he could pick up the bitch's trail—until she'd vanished into the maze of streets surrounding her house. Half of them were one-way, and that had made him lose even more time as he tried to figure out which way she'd gone.

Savagely he pounded his fists against the steering wheel, stopping only when pain shot up his arms. He'd been so close, close enough to wrap his hands around her slender white throat. Then she'd pulled that stupid trick with the barbell. He reached down to rub his gut where she'd slammed the weight into him.

He'd had plenty of time in prison to think about what her family had done to him. Today there was more damage to add to the score, and before he finished with her, he'd make sure she understood what she owed him.

He glanced back over his shoulder. No use flapping around in circles now like a chicken with its head cut off. Better to toss her house, find that letter. If she wasn't lying about that, he thought, his fists making another violent assault on the steering wheel.

Struggling to contain his fury, he took a deep breath. There was no percentage in getting riled. Anger was dangerous. So was overconfidence.

He ordered himself to relax as he thought about the good parts of their encounter. Like that trick with the voice— making her think he was her good old friend Silvio Marco. He'd always been a great mimic, and he'd had years to perfect the skill. Maybe he should have played *her* father instead of Marco. Wouldn't that have been a hoot!

He smiled as he thought about the fun he could have with her when he caught her again. But first he'd have a nice dinner and a couple of beers while he made some plans. Then he'd drive by the house and check things out. If Ms. Leonard was stupid enough to have come back, so much the better. But it didn't really matter. Either way, he'd catch up with her soon enough.

TEARS OF FRUSTRATION stung Marianne's eyes as she leaned her head against the door. Tony wasn't home. The idea flashed through her mind of driving around back and waiting for him. But she reconsidered almost immediately. He had built up a very successful import business, which meant he went on buying trips several times a year. He could be in Europe or Asia for all she knew. He could be gone for weeks.

With leaden steps she made her way back to the car and started the engine again, this time with no idea where she was going or what she was planning to do. The only thing she knew was that she had to put as much distance as she could between herself and the madman.

Dimly it registered that the sun was setting. As the sky turned navy and then black, she kept driving in a kind of trance until she saw a highway sign—and realized with a jolt of recognition that she was on Route 50, heading for the shore. For Paradise Beach, to be exact. It seemed that if she couldn't get help from Tony, her subconscious had served up this substitute—the summer place he'd inherited from his father, where she'd spent at least a month every year. It was set back from the road. Isolated. The perfect place to hide while she figured out what to do.

After filling her almost-empty gas tank at a station on the edge of town, she turned onto the two-lane country road along the Severn River and scanned the mailboxes.

When she found the one that said ''Marco'' she let out a little sigh, turned in at the drive that wound through the woods, and pulled around to the back of the comfortable white and green Victorian house. After cutting the lights, she got out and stretched her cramped muscles.

She was starting for the front walk when the powerful beam of a flashlight suddenly hit her full in the face. Blinded, she threw up her hands.

Lord, he had found her again. The madman who had been waiting for her at home. Through some evil magic, he'd figured out where she was going and had gotten here first.

Heart pounding, she was backing toward the car when a voice with a marked country twang halted her. ''This is private property, missy. What are you doing here?''

Not him. It wasn't him. That much registered in her terror-numbed mind.

''Who are you?'' the speaker demanded gruffly, the flash-light beam pinning her.

Her hand tugged convulsively at the brim of her hat. "Tony Marco's wife," she heard herself say, shocked and dismayed at the bald-faced lie that had tumbled from her mouth, yet knowing it had come from deep within her subconscious.

"Oh yeah?"

Instantly, she wished she could take it back. But she had already trapped herself, and the only thing she could do was plunge ahead and pray for the best. "Tony's meeting me here," she said, straightening her shoulders.

"You're Tony's missus? When did you get married?"

Her mind went blank, until another fib rose to her lips like a cork bobbing to the surface of a pond. "Last week."

"I've been workin' down here all month. Tony didn't mention nothing to me about getting married."

"Well, you know how he is about keeping his personal life to himself," she tossed off. At least that was true. Moving toward the front steps as if she had every right to be there, she reached for the fake rock sitting under an azalea bush. It was back farther than she expected, and she had a few bad moments as she scrabbled in the dirt. Then her fingers latched on to the rounded surface. As she extracted the key, she raised her eyes, and the man lowered the flashlight beam.

A sigh of relief trickled out of her when the key fit the lock. Without glancing over her shoulder, she marched inside, aware that he had followed.

"I'm Horace Haliday," he said as he blocked her exit from the kitchen. "Did Tony change his mind about sellin' the place?"

Horace Haliday. She remembered him now. He'd done odd jobs for Tony's father, but she hadn't seen him in years.

"We're thinking about staying," she answered, trying to decide whether to remind him who she was. Probably it was better not to get into a long discussion.

"Yeah. Well, you could get a good piece of change for

prime waterfront property. Not that you need the money with Tony doin' so well in his business and all.'' He cleared his throat. "Sorry about flashing that light in your eyes, Miz Marco. I wasn't expecting you.''

The form of address made her cringe. Lord, how was she going to worm her way out of this? Clearing her throat, she pasted a smile on her face. "I'm pretty tired. It was a long ride down from Baltimore, so I'd like to get some rest.''

He stood uncertainly in the doorway, then backed away. A few moments later, she heard a vehicle start. In the moonlight, she could see a pickup truck lumbering toward the main road.

When it was finally out of sight, she slumped against the kitchen counter and locked her knees to keep them from trembling as an instant replay of her cock-and-bull story flashed through her mind.

Tony's wife! For years that had been her secret dream. Too bad she hadn't kept it to herself.

If he ever found out, she could never look him in the eye again. For long moments she stood there with her head in her hands. But she was too wrung out to stay on her feet for long.

With a grimace, she pushed away from the counter, flipped on the light switch, and discovered that the electricity had been cut off. *Par for the course,* she thought as she rummaged in the pantry and found a flashlight. There were candles, too, but she hated open flames.

In the living room, she shined the light on the familiar surroundings, profoundly glad that nothing had changed. The place was furnished for comfort, with wicker chairs and tables and an overstuffed chintz couch set in the middle of the room, angled to provide a view of the river.

Although it was stifling inside, she was afraid to open the windows more than a crack. But her sweat-soaked dress and stockings were intolerable.

Climbing the creaking staircase to the second floor, she

hesitated in the hall, then opened the door to Tony's room. She hadn't come in here much, but she assumed he kept clothing in the dresser. When she opened the second drawer and shined the flashlight inside, she found more than clothing. A box of condoms was wedged beside a pile of underwear.

Instant heat flared in her cheeks. Snatching out a T-shirt, she shoved the drawer closed, sorry that she had invaded his privacy—and sorry that her heart had started pounding again.

Squeezing her eyes closed, she ordered herself to stop reacting like an idiot. So he'd brought girlfriends down here. Well, what of it? He was a grown man. She knew he must have had relationships with women. Yet the hard evidence wasn't something she wanted to face.

Whirling, she trotted out of the room. Too tired to search for something else to wear, she undressed in the bathroom and pulled the T-shirt over her head. It was miles too big, but the fact that it was Tony's gave her a sense of security.

Wearily she tottered down the hall and eyed the bed in the guest room, but the thought of sleeping so far from an escape route made her nervous.

Somewhere in her shell-shocked mind she knew that she shouldn't stay here. Not after that encounter with Mr. Haliday. But she was too mentally and physically exhausted to flee again. About all she could do was stagger back downstairs and huddle on the sofa with her arms wrapped around her knees, her mind blessedly numb. Soon sleep stole over her.

Sometime later, her eyes snapped open again. The heat was like an asbestos blanket lying heavily on her body, and her skin was covered with a fine sheen of perspiration. Was it the temperature that had awakened her? Or something more sinister?

Every muscle in her body rigid, she strained her ears, slitted her eyes. The flashlight she'd left on shone feebly now, but along with the moonlight filtering through the windows, the orange glow was enough to give her the outlines of the room.

Her anxious gaze probed the shadows, but nothing stirred. And no sound reached her. It must have been something outside—probably a fox or a raccoon—that had wakened her. That was all, she assured herself, trying to force her tight muscles to relax again. Feigning sleep, she shifted uneasily, all her attention focused on the darkened doorway leading to the hall.

When a floorboard creaked, she bit down on her lip to keep from crying out.

Oh, Lord. No.

The quality of the darkness changed, and she realized there was a figure blocking the entrance—a large male figure, she judged from the height of his head and the width of his shoulders. He was turned toward her, his face hidden by the shadows, but she could feel the force of his gaze pressing against her body.

The breath solidified in her lungs. Without moving, she flicked her eyes to the right and left, looking for something to use as a weapon. She found nothing.

Sheer blinding panic threatened to swallow her whole as she remembered the feel of those steely fingers squeezing her neck. A whimper rose in her throat, but she clamped it off by digging her nails into the palm of her hand. The pain cut through the fog swamping her brain.

Summoning all her resolve, she leaped up and vaulted over the sofa back—making for the rear of the house.

Behind her she heard a surprised exclamation. Then the invader was scrambling after her. Within seconds, he was on her, catching her from behind the way he had before and stopping her forward motion. His hands were on her shoulders, his supple body pressed to her back.

The position fueled her panic. Again, she couldn't see his face. All she knew was that he was strong and deadly—and he should have been able to hold her. But her strength came from desperation as she began to fight him, kicking at his legs, stamping down on his feet with all her strength.

"No," she whimpered. "No! Let me go."

As she spoke, he made a strangled sound, and his grip loosened. She hadn't really believed he would let her go. But she took advantage of the opportunity to wiggle out of his grasp. Stumbling forward, she found her footing, sprinted toward the back door, and flung it open before fleeing mindlessly into the night.

She could hardly see in the waning moonlight. But she kept running, her only goal to escape his clutches again.

"Wait! Stop." The wind caught his voice, distorting it and carrying it away.

Not in this lifetime, her mind screamed. Weeds whipped at her legs, stinging her flesh as she dashed headlong into the darkness, heedless of everything but the sound of his footsteps pounding closer.

Rough boards slapped against the bottoms of her feet. Gasping for breath, she put on a desperate burst of speed.

"No! Stop! Marianne!" He called her name, and this time the sound of his voice pulled at her, almost checking her steps. But her whole being was tuned to flight and only physical force could have stopped her.

She reached the end of the boards and went sailing into space. A scream of denial tore from her lips as she plummeted down, down—her fall broken only by bone-freezing water.

Chapter Two

Her arms flailed as dark water sucked her downward into oblivion. Then she reached the murky river bottom and reflexively pushed upward with all her might. Lungs bursting, she struggled toward the surface, hardly sure if she was moving in the right direction. Finally, finally her head broke into the cool night air, and she dragged in a gasping breath.

Swim, she ordered herself. *You can swim if you don't panic.* But the dark and the fear made her limbs stiff, and she felt herself going under again.

Beside her, the water splashed and churned, then strong hands grabbed her shoulders, and she screamed, flailing out as she tried to free herself.

She went under again, sputtering as she came up.

"Marianne, don't. It's Tony. Don't fight me, baby."

The words hardly registered as her fists pounded against his chest, pushing him down, clawing at him with the last of her strength. If she was going to drown, she would do her best to take him with her.

"I won't hurt you. Please." He was breathing hard as he pulled her roughly to her back and locked his arm across her breasts. Far stronger than she, he brought her body under control, and she sobbed in fear.

His hand tightened on her shoulder. "Don't fight me, Marianne. It's Tony," he said, over and over, his familiar voice finally cutting through the temporary insanity of her panic.

Tony. It couldn't be. Yet the reality was finally sinking in. It was Tony whose rock-hard arms held her head above the water.

The mind-numbing terror evaporated, and she went slack, except for the coughs racking her body.

"Good, that's good," he crooned, his hand touching her shoulder. "I'm going to tow you to shore. Okay?"

"Yes," she managed as he began to pull her through the water, his muscular legs kicking and his free arm stroking. Then he was stumbling onto the beach, his breath harsh in her ears as he lowered her to the sand.

She lay with her eyes closed, unable to stop coughing.

Crouching low, Tony pulled her up, draping her across his forearm and pounded on her back as she rid her lungs of river water.

"Marianne. Marianne." He said her name over and over, his tone low and urgent. "Are you okay?"

"Yes," she managed.

As her mind began to function again, she became aware of her dripping hair and the way her breasts were plastered against him. The plunge into the river had made her nipples hard, and she felt them stabbing against the shirt. *His* shirt, she suddenly remembered, keeping her face turned away from him in chagrin.

Eyes closed, she tried to put a few inches of space between them.

"Rest. Just rest." He eased her back so that her head was cradled in his lap, then pushed the wet hair away from her eyes with a touch so gentle she barely felt the pressure.

She cleared her throat as she took in her surroundings. They were on the narrow beach where she'd played as a kid. And she'd plunged off the end of the boat dock.

"Why did you run away?" he rasped.

Raising her face, she tried to read the expression in his eyes. But she couldn't penetrate the darkness or his lowered lashes.

"I...I didn't know it was you," she stammered. "You...you came at me like a—a lion bringing down its prey," she wheezed.

He rubbed a hand across his eyes. "Yeah, well, when I saw you on the couch, lying there like you owned the place, I didn't know who you were. Then you leaped up and ran. I thought—"

"What?"

"That you'd lied your way into the house and you were trying to get away when the owner showed up."

When she sucked in a sharp breath, he cupped his hand around her shoulder, the fingers pressing painfully into her flesh. "What did you expect me to think? Horace called me. Asked me if I'd gotten married. When I accused him of being drunk, he said some woman was down here posing as my wife. I don't have a wife." The last part came out gravelly and strained.

Glad that the darkness hid the rising color in her cheeks, she tried to imagine the phone call. "I shouldn't have told him that," she murmured. "It was a stupid thing to say."

"Why did you?"

She heard the stiffness in his voice, and wondered what he must think of her. Looking up at him, she became aware for the first time that he was sopping, too.

Lord, he'd come charging down here to deal with a trespasser. And what he'd gotten for his trouble was a dunk in the river rescuing a crazy woman who'd done her best to drown him.

Thoroughly mortified, she pushed herself off the ground and tried to cover her naked thighs by tugging at the hem of the shirt. She stopped when she saw from the corner of her eye that he was watching her intently—and that she was probably making things worse, if modesty was her intention.

"Baby, take it easy. Tell me why you came down here."

At the moment, she didn't trust her voice, so she gave him a quick shake of the head and wheeled toward the house, wincing when the bottom of her foot slapped down on a sharp piece of gravel.

TONY RAN HIS HAND through his wet hair, then strode after her. God, he was so off balance he was asking her all the wrong questions. But as soon as he'd gotten off the phone with Horace, he'd leaped into his car and sped down here fully prepared to do battle with a sneak thief or worse. Instead he'd found Marianne Leonard—so frightened that she'd fought her way out of the house and dashed headlong into the river.

Either she had figuratively gone off the deep end, or... It was the "or" that made the hairs on the back of his neck prickle. Marianne Leonard was one of the most steady, reliable people he'd ever met. If she was scared out of her mind, then something pretty bad had happened—and he had to find out what it was.

He watched her marching toward the house, her wet T-shirt and panties revealing every breathtaking line of her lithe body. The sight made him respond the way he'd been responding to her since her shape had changed from child to woman—with a quick, predictable zing of sexual awareness that he always fought to repress.

Usually he coped by putting some distance between them. Tonight that wasn't going to be an option. Not when she was strung as tightly as a wire about to snap. Not when she so obviously needed his help.

In a few quick strides, he caught up with her. "Marianne. Wait."

"I didn't mean to make trouble for you," she whispered,

her head down, tears edging her voice as she marched toward the porch. "I'm sorry about telling Horace that stupid story. And I'm sorry you got wet. I'll clear out as soon as I change."

"No." The self-accusation in her voice was like a lash against his skin. Catching hold of her arm, he pulled her toward him, feeling the stiffness of her muscles as she resisted any attempt at comfort from him.

"Marianne, baby. Don't run away from me now," he muttered, folding her against his chest, cupping the back of her head and bringing her face against his shoulder.

For endless seconds she stood as unyielding as a department-store mannequin. Then her entire body began to shake.

"Ah, baby, don't," he crooned. "It's okay. Everything is going to be okay."

"No," she said again, the tiny syllable laced with tears that she was struggling to contain.

"Whatever it is, we'll deal with it," he murmured as he held her in the moonlight, stroking his fingers across her back, trying to comfort and calm her.

When she lost the struggle for control and began to sob in his arms, all the tender emotions he had tried to keep in check where she was concerned swept over him like a flood tide.

One hand caressed the damp strands of her hair. He couldn't see them in the darkness, but he knew they were like spun gold, heating his fingers even wet from the river. He couldn't see her face, either, but it didn't matter. He had already committed the details to memory—the small pouty mouth, the sea-green eyes with lashes and brows several shades darker than her hair, the ivory skin. The totality added up to an enticing picture that had captivated him long ago.

His other hand smoothed over her shoulders, then down her spine, setting off a little shiver in her body that transmitted itself to his. How long had it been since he'd let himself hold her like this, he wondered, his senses dazed by the feel of her, the scent, the warmth of her skin.

Never. Never precisely like this.

Unable to check himself, he turned his head, his lips skimming the tender edge of her cheek. It was soft and dewy like a flower petal.

She had stopped crying, her feminine body pliant in his embrace, her hand moving restlessly across his back. Somewhere along the line he forgot why he was cradling her in his arms—his only conscious thought was that she was finally where she belonged.

Even through their wet clothes, the heat of her body seared him, the imprint of her breasts against his chest and the pressure of her hips against his promising untold delights. He wanted more, needed more.

His own body hardened in helpless arousal, and when his hand slid downward to cup her sweetly rounded bottom and pull her against his swollen flesh, she made a small sound and moved against him as though they'd practiced these moves a thousand times.

Only in his dreams.

But this was no dream, and the reality of her eager response brought him back to his senses. What the hell was he doing? He'd sworn never to touch her like this, but when he'd taken her into his arms, he'd thrown every good intention out the window.

While he could still command his mind to work, he eased her body away from his, sucking in a strangled gasp of cold night air as he tried to gather his scattered wits.

She tipped her face upward, her parted lips inches from his. For a moment he couldn't move, couldn't do more than stare at her quivering mouth, imagining the taste of her, the warmth, the wet stroking of his tongue against her inner lips.

Then he shook himself, knowing he could never have the very thing he longed for most in the world.

"Marianne," he managed. "Come inside. You have to change before you catch your death of cold."

"Cold?" she answered, the puzzlement in her voice rich and vibrant. "I'm not cold."

"I am," he lied, turning and making for the steps, giving her a gentle tug. "You'll feel better when you've washed off the river water. Then you can tell me why you came down here."

He guided her into the house, then let go of her hand before striding to the breaker box in the utility room and switching on the electricity. When he returned to the living room, she was blinking in the sudden brightness. Tempted past good manners, he allowed his eyes one hot sweep over the curves of her body, barely hidden by the wet, clinging T-shirt. His T-shirt, he assumed from the size.

His hot gaze traveled upward and focused on a patch of red spread across her right cheek. From his beard. His brand. *Damn.*

She looked away, as if her thoughts were following the same track. He watched her eyes darting around the room, searching for a point of focus—and knew to the heartbeat when she discovered the gun he'd set on the coffee table before charging after her.

She made a little wheezing sound, her gaze shooting back to his face. "Were you planning to shoot somebody?"

"No. But I was prepared for trouble." Crossing the room, he picked up the weapon and casually slipped it into the end-table drawer, out of sight.

"Are you always prepared for trouble?"

"Yeah," he answered, wondering if she had caught the wealth of meaning in his answer. He'd been waiting for trouble since he was a kid. And he had the sudden, almost preternatural conviction that it had finally found him—found both of them.

Or was he letting his runaway imagination overcome his judgment? If he tried hard, he could come up with a couple of scenarios for why she'd fled down here. But until she told him the reason for her panic, there was no point in making assumptions.

When her eyes went back to the drawer, he cleared his throat. "I'll get you something dry to wear. You can change in the bathroom. Then we'll talk."

She pulled her gaze away from the end table, but kept her face averted. "Okay," she finally answered. "I guess I owe you that much."

He wanted to tell her she didn't owe him a damn thing. Instead he stood there staring at her pale face and huge eyes, aching to fold her back into his arms and feel her body pressed to the length of his again.

Shaking himself out of the trance, he turned and made for the stairs, taking them two at a time. In his room, he found more of his clothes for her—a green T-shirt and shorts. He even remembered to add a towel, which he laid on the sink, along with the clothing.

For himself he grabbed a blue button-down shirt and cut-off jeans. When he heard her close the bathroom door, he went downstairs and through the kitchen, to the outdoor shower enclosure they used to wash the sand off when they came back from the river. It was cold. But cold was what he needed.

After stripping off his sodden slacks and shirt, he turned the tap and stepped under the icy spray, tipping his face up to wash away the heat from his cheeks.

LIKE HE'D PLANNED, Arlan Duvalle had come back to the Leonard house. Now he waited in the shadows, his attention trained on the darkened windows.

Leonard. You'd think the widow could have come up with a name that was a little more imaginative. But that was typical of her mentality. She'd been a stubborn cow of a woman, always whining and complaining and bitching at her poor husband.

Really, the bastard was better off in his grave.

"Leonard. And Marco." This time he said it in an angry parody of Bobby St. Paul's voice, another voice from the past. The kids might have new names, but he had found them anyway. Too bad the senior Marco was dead, along with his pal, St. Paul. One less score to settle. But the two kids would do. All these years they thought they'd gotten away free and clear. Now it was time to settle up.

Finding them had taken money, a good part of the stash he'd hidden before the law had caught up with him. But he wasn't worried about that at the moment.

Satisfied that little Miss Leonard hadn't called the cops, he slipped through the shadows to the back door where he'd gotten in the first time. He was amused that she hadn't invested in a decent dead bolt—although it wouldn't have stopped him for long.

It had been easy to get in. It was easier now, because nobody had come back to lock the door. Slipping inside, he stood in the kitchen listening, watching. But everything was still and quiet.

Clicking on his flashlight, he aimed it at the floor. He'd learned the layout of the house on one of his previous visits, so he headed straight for the little room down the hall that she used as an office. Maybe the letter from her father was there. Or maybe it was in her room. If it was here, he'd find it.

MARIANNE HAD HEARD guys joke about cold showers. She hadn't figured she'd need one—until tonight.

One moment she'd been crying in Tony's arms like a

bedraggled little kid. Then she'd stopped crying and begun to pay attention to the touch of his hands on her back, the pressure of his hips against hers, the heat leaping between them.

All this time, she'd thought he wasn't attracted to her, but tonight had changed her perspective. The flow of electricity between them hadn't all been one-sided. The hot current had come from him as well as herself. Or was she so unhinged that she was reading things into his comforting touch that weren't intended?

Stepping out of the shower, she gave an unconscious little shrug. She might not be sure of herself when it came to man-woman responses. But she was darn sure about the wild tale she'd told to Mr. Haliday. She'd claimed to be Tony's wife. Now she was going to have to explain that to the man who was supposed to be her husband.

Lifting her head, she stared at her face in the mirror, at her wide eyes and the color staining her cheeks. It was partly from embarrassment—and partly from where Tony's beard had burned her flesh when he'd moved his cheek against hers.

Delicately, she ran her fingers over the tingling skin. After everything that had happened, the thought of confronting him again was simply too much. Maybe she could get out of here, make it to her car before he realized she was gone.

But then what? The madman was out there. Although facing Tony might be humiliating, it was better than getting strangled. However, her nerves were too raw to expose herself quite yet, so she snatched up the towel and began to dry her hair, rubbing it until her arms ached.

When he called her name from the bottom of the stairs, she jumped.

"Marianne? Are you all right up there?"

She cleared her throat to steady her voice. "Yes."

"Then come down."

"In a minute," she answered, wondering how she was going to get through the next half hour.

Silently she descended the steps, grateful that he'd turned off most of the overhead lights. In the glow from a couple of lamps, she could see him pacing back and forth between the sofa and the window.

"I'm a mess," she whispered when he stopped and gave her a long look, his expression tight.

"You're fine," he said in a clipped tone, and she was instantly sure that she had imagined his response to her after the river. This was the old Tony. The man who deliberately kept her at arm's length—unless she needed his help. Which was definitely the case tonight.

He'd changed into cutoffs that hugged his narrow hips and an old blue shirt that defined the broad expanse of his shoulders. But his lean cheeks were dark with the day's growth of beard that had stung her skin.

Stiffly, she perched on the edge of the couch, her fingers twisting the hem of her second borrowed T-shirt of the day. Although he'd opened the windows wide, and the room was a little cooler, she felt a trickle of sweat rolling down her neck.

Desperately, she tried to distance herself from him, but couldn't prevent a treacherous thought from stealing into her mind. If she were his wife, then this would be their honeymoon. But if he were her new husband, he would have shaved so that his beard wouldn't do any more damage to her skin when he—

Appalled by that dangerous line of thinking, she compressed her lips.

Unfortunately, he picked that moment to glance up, his gaze drawn to her mouth as he took several slow steps toward the couch. Before reaching her, he stopped and shook his head as if to clear it.

"Marianne, whatever it is, we'll deal with it," he said in a thick voice.

She sighed inwardly. At least he hadn't caught the drift of her thoughts. Had he? Determined not to make an even bigger fool of herself than she already had, she tried to focus on something besides the way his tall male body dominated her vision. But it was impossible to stop herself from taking in the details. Apparently he hadn't found a replacement for his waterlogged shoes because his feet were bare. So were hers, and somehow that made the encounter more intimate. Pulling up her legs, she tucked her feet under her body and searched for a safe place to center her gaze.

It landed on a can of soda on the glass-topped wicker coffee table. Her favorite brand, she noted, as she picked it up and wiped the beads of moisture forming on the outside. When she realized that Tony was watching her intently, she took a quick sip to moisten her dry mouth.

"Start from the beginning," he ordered, then began pacing the room again. "Tell me why you're hiding out down here."

She rolled the can between her hands. "It's cold," she whispered. "I thought the electricity was off."

"I got it from Horace's ice chest. Now quit stalling and tell me what happened to you." His eyes turned fierce. "Was it some guy?"

When she blinked at him, he continued with repressed anger. "Did some guy you were dating hurt you? If he did, I'll kill him!"

The violent reaction brought her head up sharply. "It's nothing like that." She gulped a swallow of soda and almost choked. "At least, not what you're thinking."

"Then what? Marianne, you can trust me."

"I know," she answered, then forced herself to start speaking. "When—when I got home tonight, there was a man in my house. Some of the time he sounded plain crazy.

And some of the time he acted like he knew me—like I should know *him*."

Stopping in midstride, Tony whirled toward her, his eyes burning into hers. "What man? What did he look like?"

"He didn't want me to see him. He held my back to his front." Clutching the soda can, she went on. "He said I knew some secret. That my father had told me something." She spread her hands, mystified. "I never knew my father. But this guy thought I did. He said if I didn't tell him what he wanted to know, he—he was going to kill me."

She almost jumped off the couch as Tony's fist came smashing down against the sideboard. "Tell me everything you remember!" he demanded. "Everything he said."

"I—I thought he'd escaped from a lunatic asylum. Are you saying I'm supposed to know him?"

"Yes! Dammit."

She'd wanted to believe she was a random victim. Somehow that had given her a measure of safety. Tony's savage reaction extinguished that dim hope. When she lost the battle to keep from shaking, he came and sat down beside her on the couch, turning her so that he could cradle her close.

"Who is he?" she whispered. "I don't even know what he wants."

"He won't touch you again," he vowed, and she clung to the assurance in his voice.

His hand kneaded the tight muscles of her back. "Tell me the rest," he said more gently. "All of it. I need to know exactly what happened."

Hesitantly she began to give him the details. When she got to the part about the attacker sounding like his father, Tony cursed. "The bastard!"

Next she told him about the barbell, and his hand squeezed her shoulder. "Good. Good for you!"

Finally, she ran out of words and slumped against him,

exhausted. Yet she felt the tension radiating from his arms, from his whole body.

"Duvalle," he ground out.

"Who?"

"It has to be Duvalle," he repeated the unfamiliar name. "That's the only thing that makes sense. Imitating my dad's voice sounds like his sick sense of humor."

"None of it makes sense!" she almost shouted, pushing herself away from him. "I don't have a clue about what he wanted!"

He angled his upper body so he could meet her eyes. "That name doesn't mean anything to you?"

She shook her head, yet somewhere in the back of her mind, memories prickled like ants creeping along her skin.

His eyes drilled into her, and she wanted to hide from him—from herself. But she could see he wasn't going to let her duck away from this, whatever it was.

"How long have we known each other?" he asked.

She made a rapid calculation. "Eighteen years."

"It's longer than that," he growled, leaving her no room for argument.

When she shook her head helplessly, he watched her like a hawk watching a rabbit.

"Look, we never talked about it, but you were five when you moved to Baltimore. You must have *some* specific memories from before that," he prodded. "What about your fifth birthday party? Most kids remember birthdays. Christmas? Don't you remember the dollhouse you wanted so badly?"

She could only stare at him.

"You were real sick with the chicken pox. Then when you felt better, you sneaked downstairs and ate a box of chocolates. Or what about that stuffed bear you used to drag around everywhere you went? Don't you remember that your dad gave it to you?"

An image of her beloved Mr. Edgar flashed into her mind. She'd clung to the bear like a security blanket until it had literally fallen apart. But she didn't remember who'd given it to her—not on a conscious level, anyway. Raising her shoulders, she shrugged, although this time she felt the teeth of nightmares nipping her cold flesh.

"Okay," he said, in a weary voice, then dug his hands into the pockets of his cutoffs. Through the worn fabric, she could see that his hands were clenched into tight fists. She felt the waves of tension radiating from him and wanted to shout at him to get on with it—whatever *it* was. But she knew that making demands would get her nowhere. Tony Marco had never let himself be pushed.

Finally, he sighed. "There's no way to make this pretty— so I'll say it straight out. My father and yours robbed liquor stores. Then banks."

She tried for a laugh, but it came out high and false. "Tony, you're kidding me."

"No joke," he bit out. "The really hellish part came when they took on another partner—a bastard named Arlan Duvalle. I know they were sorry about getting hooked up with him—especially after he went crazy and shot a bank teller."

Stunned, she could only stare at him. "What are you saying?"

"The truth," he spat out. "Your dad and mine were best buddies—and damn criminals. That's how they supported their families—until it all blew up in their faces."

Chapter Three

"No!" Marianne cried out again, twisting away from him. Springing off the couch, she stood in the center of the room trembling, her skin suddenly icy. "My mother said…"

Tony climbed to his feet, his jaw tight, his hands balled at his sides. "Forget everything your mother told you about your dad. Did you ever ask her why she despised *my* father so much? Did you ever ask her why she'd warned you to stay away from me?"

"You knew that?"

"Of course."

She looked down, unable to meet the fierce challenge in his gaze. Her mother had been so closed, so angry about certain subjects that asking questions had been impossible. So she had never tried to find out why nice Mr. Marco was on Mom's blacklist. Still, the questions lingered in her mind: If Mom hated Mr. Marco so much, why did they see him all the time? Why did she let him do things for them and help out with expenses? Why did Mom let her come down here every summer for a vacation? Why did Mom act like Tony would protect her—while at the same time warning her not to get involved with him?

It hadn't made sense. Yet there was a lot about Mom's own private rules for living that hadn't stood up to close scrutiny. Marianne had learned that it was sometimes prudent to keep her thoughts to herself, and life with Mom hadn't really been bad—just a tad strange.

Tony was speaking again, his voice flat and dead, in sharp contrast to the anger flashing in his eyes. "Your dad and mine were two grunts who came home from Vietnam and couldn't get jobs because half of society was down on vets. For months they sat around the living room drinking beer and complaining about how the country owed them a living. Then my dad got the brilliant idea that they should take what they deserved. From their point of view, it all worked out okay for a while." Tony stood there, his mouth twisted in disgust. "Now their partner Arlan Duvalle is out of prison and looking for—" He stopped, and opened his palms. "Revenge."

"Revenge for what?"

"He was the only one of the three the police caught."

"But why did he come after me?"

"*You and me*," he corrected sharply. "Because we're the only ones left." He raked a hand through his dark hair. "I knew *something* was going on these past couple of weeks. I just didn't know what." His head jerked toward her. "Did you get the feeling someone was checking up on you, poking into your business?"

She made a small sound. "I felt like someone was following me. Then I'd look up, and nobody would be there." Helplessly, she gestured with her hands. "I was scared. But I couldn't figure out what was going on."

"You should have come to me."

She felt her jaw muscles tighten. "Come on, Tony. You haven't exactly invited me over in the past few years."

His eyes took on a haunted look. "If I'd thought you were in trouble, I would have been there. All you had to do was ask."

She crossed to the window and stared out into the darkness, unable to tell him she'd been too proud to come begging—until the attack had changed everything.

Everything—because she understood now, deep in her bones, that the framework of her life had been shattered like a crystal bowl struck by a hammer. As she raised her eyes again and stared at Tony's bleak face she knew something else as well.

"You've been expecting this," she breathed. "All these years, you've been waiting for him to come back."

"No," he said, then sighed. "Okay. Yes. In the back of my mind I knew he held a grudge. From his twisted perspective, he had valid reasons. But I thought my dad might have done a good enough job of hiding our identities."

"And you didn't want me to know about any of it," she added, watching his eyes, searching for new truths.

"I didn't figure he was going to come after *you!* I assumed I'd be the target, and I thought I could handle him. Apparently I underestimated his devious mind."

For long moments she stood listening to the blood pounding in her veins. Her father and Tony's had been criminals. And Tony and everyone else had hidden the truth from her.

"You've had eighteen years of peace," he said, his voice very quiet. "Now you have to remember what your life was like before you came to Baltimore."

"Why?"

His tone turned fierce. "Because something happened the night it all went to hell. Something between you and your father. Or your father and Duvalle. And you've got to figure out what it was."

"I don't know *anything!*" she flung at him. "*You* have to tell *me!*"

He shook his head. "I wish I could, but I wasn't there. I was out with your mother at a drugstore getting bandages and painkillers for your father."

She jerked around to face him. "My father," she

wheezed as another detail shifted in her mind. "Wait a minute. What are you saying? I thought my father left us when I was a baby. That's what Mom always told me. Now you're saying that isn't true?"

Tony shook his weary head. "No. But maybe it would have been better if he had."

Reaching behind her, she gripped the window ledge to steady herself. "It's hard to believe all this," she whispered.

Tony took a step toward her. In a deceptively quiet voice, he asked, "Did you ever wonder why you're afraid of fire?"

The mere question brought a choking sensation to her chest, even as an automatic denial sprang to her lips. "No."

"Don't lie to me! At least, don't lie."

"Why not? You lied to me. For years you lied to me. From what you're telling me, everybody lied."

"We did it for your own good! When we first got to Baltimore, we were all living in the same rented house, and you used to wake up screaming in your bed. When the nightmares stopped, we all breathed a sigh of relief. Lots of times I wanted to ask if you remembered anything, but I never did."

Turning away, she held on to the window ledge for dear life. The nightmares hadn't stopped. They had never stopped—not entirely.

"It all ended in a fire," Tony said, his voice low and urgent as he stood in back of her, blocking her escape. "You were in the middle of it. Maybe you've shut it out of your conscious mind, but it's there—somewhere!"

Against her will, visions of an inferno flickered at the edge of her awareness. When she shuddered, he stroked her arms, and she knew he could feel the goose bumps. "It's all right. I'll keep you safe."

Memories beckoned—but they were just beyond her grasp. Were they real, or had he planted them in her mind with his wild stories about outlaw parents and a conflagration?

His father and hers. Bank robbers. And their careers had ended in a blaze of fire.... No, he couldn't have made that up.

For years, it had been a secret locked behind a steel door in her mind. Tony's words had opened the door a crack and beyond it was a vision of hell.

Against her will, the door flew open—revealing the dancing flames in all their terror. She tried to slam the door closed, but it was too late. She was swept back in time—suddenly immersed in the awful heat. "Fire," she gasped. "There was fire all around me."

Tony's hands tightened on her shoulders, and she moaned, trying to twist out of his grasp.

He held her fast, his body like a shield in the inferno. "It's okay. It was a long time ago. It can't hurt you now."

He was wrong. It could hurt her. She had always known it could hurt her. She had awakened from dreams choking, gasping for breath, her lungs on fire and her eyes stinging. But as she'd lain shaking in her bed, she had never cried out for her mother—lest she find out where the nightmare came from.

Today a man named Duvalle had snatched away her security blanket. Still caught in the flickering memories, her mind spun back to the heat, the fear as fire raged around her. Then someone was picking her up, cradling her in his arms, pulling her to safety. Someone bigger than she—but not a man. A boy, she suddenly realized.

Pivoting, she faced Tony, her expression gravely serious as she focused on his broad chest. "Why did you always wear a T-shirt when we went swimming?" she asked.

He didn't answer.

Slowly she raised her hands to his shirt front and slipped

her fingers under the placket so that she could feel warm skin and crisp hair.

"Don't," he warned, taking a quick step back.

But this time she wasn't taking orders from him or anyone else. With deliberate care, she closed the distance he'd put between them, then began to slide open the buttons of his shirt, her fingers not quite steady as she bared his chest.

Under her hand she could feel his heart racing. It matched the frantic pounding of hers. She kept her eyes down, unable to meet his beseeching gaze as she pushed back the edges of the shirt, exposing his well-muscled chest. Dark hair spread across it, swirled around his nipples, arrowed downward toward his abdomen.

Yet near his right shoulder was a patch of rough, red skin where the hair didn't grow. She touched the broad scar, feeling his flesh quiver beneath her fingertips.

As her hands made a foray over his warm skin, she was caught in a web of emotions—frightening memories at war with sensual awareness. Astonished at her own boldness, yet unable to change her course of action, she pushed the shirt off his wide shoulders, revealing more scars. Reaching higher, she traced the line of his collarbone, then slid her hands to his back—where her questing fingers found another place with the same roughened flesh.

He didn't move, didn't pull away.

"You were burned," she said, her voice barely above a whisper.

His lips moved, but he didn't answer.

"You were burned rescuing me," she gasped out. "That's what happened all those years ago, didn't it?"

"Yes!" He flung that one syllable at her, then wrenched himself away. But she only reached for him, pulled him back into the charged space that seemed to enclose them.

Her eyes squeezed shut, she pressed her face against his

skin, feeling the rapid rise and fall of his chest. "You could have gotten killed."

"I had to get you out of there," he rasped, every muscle in his body rigid with the tension that arced between them.

"Tell me what happened."

"We were on the run, and we were spending the night in an abandoned house. When your mom and I got back from the store, we could see the flames shooting into the air. I jumped out of the car and ran to the house and saw you in there, crying, choking, trying to get out."

Her face moved against his broad chest, letting the deep thumping of his heart sink into her flesh. Into her soul. Turning her head, she trailed her lips against him. "You should have told me."

"I couldn't."

To protect her—or himself?

She let go of the question as his hand stroked her hair, gently, the barest whisper of a touch, yet the contact was strong enough to send a vibration through her.

Breathing in his familiar scent, she dared to touch her tongue to his crinkly hair and heated skin. She should move away, stop touching him like this. Yet now that she had dared so much, her legs wouldn't cooperate.

A strange sense of power and weakness fought for dominance within her—aided and abetted by the knowledge that the intimacy was affecting him as powerfully as he was affecting her. This time, she was sure. This wasn't just *her* fantasy come to life. *His* body had tightened, hardened, in response to her touch.

Slowly she raised her face to his. His hands clasped her shoulder, drawing her toward him, pressing the length of her body to his. She melted into his embrace, closing her eyes as she simply absorbed this new level of awareness between them while his arms drew her closer, then closer still.

When he had her where he wanted her, his hold shifted, his hands splaying across her ribs, exploring their delicate ridges, sending ripples of sensation coursing through her. The hands stole inward, the sides of his thumbs finding the lower curve of her breasts. A sound of wanting welled in her throat as she waited for him to cup her, mold her.

When he did, it was like a thousand tiny shocks electrifying her nerve endings.

"Tony," she breathed.

"Ah, baby. You feel so good."

"Yes. Oh, yes."

He seemed to read her mind, seemed to know that she wanted his fingers to circle her nipples, to stroke them, squeeze them so that heat shot downward through her body.

Earlier she had boldly said she was his wife. If they were husband and wife, there would be nothing wrong with touching each other like this—this and a lot more.

Before she could wrap her mind around the thought, his hands dropped away from her breasts, leaving them hot and aching with need. When she tried to reach for him again, he took a step back and shook his head. "We can't."

"Why not?" she asked, trying and failing to come up with one valid reason. They both wanted this—and more. Much more.

Yet the look in his eyes wasn't what she expected. They brimmed with an anguish that stole the breath from her lungs. "Tony?"

He made a low sound in his throat. "We have to talk. About Duvalle. We have to figure out what he wants and how he's planning to get it."

True enough, she agreed silently, fighting to take hold of reality. Somewhere along the line, she had forgotten why they were standing there with his shirt unbuttoned and their bodies hot and aching. But she also knew from the set of his mouth that he was reaching for excuses to distance himself from her again. So much for her fantasies.

When he began to button his shirt, she turned her head away. Keeping her gaze down, she walked stiffly to the couch again and sat. He stayed behind her, out of her line of vision. Maybe he didn't even know that he was hiding from her, but she understood. Too much was happening between them. Not just the sudden flare of sexual need. In the space of half an hour, their whole relationship had changed—and neither of them knew how to cope with it. But there was one thing she knew for sure. It was time for the truth, the whole truth. "What happened to my father?" she demanded.

"He...he died in the fire."

"Why? Why couldn't he get away?" she pushed.

When he didn't answer immediately, she pounded her hand on the coffee table, making the soda can jump. "You started this! You have to finish it."

"Okay, I guess you need to know how it went down," he agreed, sounding weary. "I already told you Duvalle started a shoot-out at the bank where they'd gone to make an unscheduled withdrawal."

When she nodded tightly, he went on. "Your father took a bullet in the shoulder."

Though she winced, he kept talking.

"My dad grabbed him and dragged him to the car. The two of them drove back to the house where your mother was waiting with us. Duvalle came roaring up just as they were ready to leave. Maybe he'd decided to split, then changed his mind."

Marianne tried to imagine the horror and confusion of the scene as Tony continued. "We left most of our stuff and piled into the car and the station wagon. That night we had to stop because your father wasn't fit to travel. Something happened while I was gone. By the time I got back, the house was on fire. I got you out. Duvalle escaped, but he was captured later. Your father never got out of the house.''

She sat staring into space, trying to absorb the terse explanation. All her life she'd believed a different story. Mom had told her that Dad had abandoned them.

Maybe from her point of view, it was true.

IN A STRANGE WAY it was a relief to have finally come clean with Marianne. Now Tony didn't have to watch his step with her, guard every word lest he give away the dirty little secret that he'd shared with her mother and his father. Still, seeing the pain and uncertainty in her eyes tore at him.

"I'm sorry you had to find out like this," he said, coming around to the front of the couch.

"My father," she said, experimenting with the words. "I have no memories of him. Now all I've got is the story of a terrible death." She swallowed convulsively, then pleaded, "Tell me something good about him."

"He cared about you and your mother. He was a good father—kind, loving. He used to tell you stories and take you places like the zoo and the park. You loved him. But you made yourself forget, and your mother helped the process along."

"She hated him."

"Take it from me, living with two guys hiding out from the law wasn't much fun. We had to be careful what we said. We couldn't make friends. We couldn't even go to the grocery story without checking our cover story. If anybody asked me questions, I'd be drilled on the correct answers."

"Oh, Tony, that must have been…" she fumbled for words. "Hard."

"Yeah."

Another basic question struck her. "Why were they dragging us around with them? Why didn't they have us live somewhere safe?"

"There was no one Dad could leave me with. And your mother wanted to stay with your father. God knows why, since she was always—" He stopped, wondering how much to say.

"Complaining?" Marianne asked.

"Right."

"Are you tactfully trying to say that she treated my father the way she treated yours?"

"Yes. She was needy and dependent—and afraid to try to make it on her own. And when things weren't going her way, she got depressed."

Marianne's vision turned inward as she remembered those characteristics. Tony was right, but it wasn't the whole story, and she desperately wanted him to understand better. "Life with Mom was never easy, but at least I knew the bottom line was that she loved me and she was doing her best to cope. I knew she wanted me to be happy. I knew she was in my corner when it counted."

"I could see that," he acknowledged.

She gave him a little nod. "I could tell it was different for you. I knew your father was hard on you, but I didn't understand why. Were you angry—like my mother?"

His eyes narrowed. "I wasn't obsessed with the past, if that's what you mean. I was too busy trying to deal with my old man on a day-to-day basis. I know my father liked to play Mr. Nice Guy with you, maybe because he wanted to make up for your not having a dad. With me, it was different. He beat the crap out of me if I got in trouble, even cursed—anything that made him think I was going to turn to a life of crime. He had impossible standards for me." He laughed sharply, bitterly. "But he bought this place with stolen money. How's that for family values?"

When she couldn't dredge up an answer, he plowed ahead. "He didn't need to hold me to a standard! I have my own values. And they're a lot higher than his ever were." He struggled to bring his roiling emotions under control. "At first I understood why he kept some of the money. He paid a lot to establish new identities for all of us. Your mother, you, me, himself."

"What do you mean—new identities?"

"New names. New backgrounds. Documents to back them up. His name used to be Vance Rossi. I suppose you don't remember calling him Uncle Vance?"

When she shook her head, he went on. "Your parents were Robert and Jeanette St. Paul. You were Margaret. Now you're Marianne Leonard—with a birth certificate and social-security number to prove it. I've even got fake school records in the name of Tony Marco."

He found that watching her try to take it in was too painful, so he moved to the bookcase, his gaze fixed on the darkened windows across the room.

She lifted her head toward him. "Who were you?" she murmured.

"Nick."

She said the name aloud. Then the others. After several seconds of silence, her shoulders rose in a little shrug. "They don't mean anything."

"Margaret doesn't sound vaguely familiar?" he pressed. "The little girl I carried out of the fire was Margaret."

"I'm sorry. I don't remember the name." Her voice quavered, and he cursed himself for not playing fair. God, she'd been to the depths of hell today, and she was trying to climb back onto solid ground. Instead of helping her, he was blocking her escape. Yet he needed information if he was going to save her from Arlan Duvalle—because her buried memories were the key to her own salvation.

Levering himself away from the bookcase, he crouched down in front of her, so that his face was level with hers. Her skin was pale and pinched, her hands clasped together so tightly that the knuckles were white, and he realized that he'd pushed her to the end of her endurance—maybe even to the end of his. He longed to offer her some comfort. There was none he could give. Except maybe the chance to escape from the pressure he was exerting on her—at least for a while.

"You need some sleep."

She gave him a tight, grateful nod. When she didn't move, he wondered if she was planning to flop back down on the sofa where he'd found her when he first came in.

"You can take your old bedroom," he said.

With a sigh she heaved herself up, and when she swayed on her feet, he moved swiftly and caught her. Effortlessly he supported her weight and for a moment she leaned into him. Then she pushed away and wove toward the steps without looking back—and he knew that she was hurting more than she wanted to admit.

ARLAN STOOD in the center of the ruined bedroom, breathing hard, his hands clenching and unclenching. He'd torn the house apart—starting with the obvious places. Then he'd gone on to the rest, growing more frustrated as he finished with each room. There was no escaping the truth. Little Miss Leonard had lied to him through her perfect white teeth. There hadn't been any letter from her father. She'd told him that so she could get away.

With a vile curse he kicked at a drawer that he'd dumped onto the floor, caving in the side. The splintering sound gave him a moment's satisfaction. Picking up a little china dog, he hurled it at the wall and watched it shatter into jagged pieces.

If he had her here he would do the same to her. Marianne Leonard, who used to be Margaret St. Paul. The daughter of the dearly departed, Bobby St. Paul.

He snorted, then said the names aloud, using first one voice and then another. Bobby and his partner Vance Rossi had been family men, afraid to take chances until they'd hooked up with him, and he'd taught them to think big. It had worked out real good. Real good. Until that lamebrain bank guard had lost his cool and gone for his gun.

Arlan squeezed his eyes shut, trying to blot out the scene in that suburban Pennsylvania bank. But it was fixed in his memory, burned into his brain. The flash of movement to his right, the guard's hand on the gun. His own hand quicker with his automatic pistol.

He'd fired first. Like in an Old West gunfight. The guard had gone down, but he'd brought down St. Paul with him. Rossi had grabbed his friend and run.

And of all the dumb bad luck, Arlan had been the one who ended up getting caught and put away. But now he was out, and he was going to get even. Anger flashed through him again. When he was calm enough to think straight, he pulled out the little spiral notebook where he'd been keeping notes. Sitting down comfortably in one of her kitchen chairs, he flipped the book open. Chapter One: "The Life of Marianne Leonard."

She worked at a nonprofit organization called the Light Street Foundation. And he'd done some research on them. Some of her co-workers had money. Some were tied into a protection service called Randolph Security. If she'd gone to them, he was in trouble. But he didn't think so. His guess was that she'd run straight into the arms of her friend Tony Marco. And if she had, he had a decent chance of finding them both—and killing two birds with one stone.

He'd also dug into Marco's import-export business, looking for a weakness he could exploit. The kid was doing pretty well for himself—and keeping his nose clean. Strange that Vance Rossi's son would be so scrupulous about morality—especially in a business where you could make big bucks by slipping stuff past customs. Either he was afraid to get on the wrong side of the law, or he was a nut. Either way, he was a chump who deserved whatever he got.

Arlan pushed himself out of the chair and walked to the door, his shoes crunching on broken crockery and the scattered contents of cereal boxes. His next step was Marco's house. If Leonard and Marco weren't there, he'd enjoy a little more constructive demolition.

MARIANNE MADE IT to the bedroom and pushed open the window, letting blessedly cool night air into the stifling room. Weaving her way to the bed, she pulled down the covers, profoundly grateful that she didn't have to go hunting for sheets and pillowcases. Pausing to strip off her borrowed shorts, she eased onto the mattress.

Since childhood, she'd never been able to sleep without something over her—even on the hottest nights. Instinctively, she burrowed under the sheet, the covering a small protection from the terrors of the night. Now at least she knew where her nightmares came from.

As she lay in the darkness, she strained her ears, hearing Tony come up the stairs and move down the hall. Apparently, her traitorous mind wasn't willing to let go of the husband-and-wife theme, maybe because it was a lot more appealing than the night's revelations of murder and fire. Mentally, she pictured Tony walking into her bedroom— and followed his arrival with an image so sexually explicit that she kicked the sheet away from her suddenly overheated body.

She pressed her palms over her face, then dug the heels of her hands into her eyes, trying to wipe out the picture of her body twined with his.

His wife. Fat chance.

Irony made her mouth twist. She had always felt a kind of secret bond with him. Tonight he'd finally told her what it was, and she'd learned she was forever tied to a life he had despised. Every moment with her was a reminder of it. No wonder he had kept his distance from her these past few years.

But it wasn't her fault, she silently railed. She hadn't done anything wrong. Neither had he. They had both been kids, dragged into a murky whirlpool of events by the adults who should have been protecting them. Until tonight, the horror had been in the past. Now it had come back to haunt them both.

She might have wept then, if she had been sure Tony wouldn't hear her. What she needed was to get away from him, where she could think, where proximity wouldn't torture them both. Yet Duvalle was out there in the night, searching for her. He had attacked her, and he might come after Tony if he couldn't get to her. So her only option was to stay and try and figure out the puzzle of her life.

But not until tomorrow. Tonight she was too wrung out to think.

Sleep claimed her once again that evening, and sometime later, a dream grabbed her by the throat.

She was a little girl, frightened and alone, wandering through the empty rooms of a dilapidated house, her terror growing as she realized everyone had gone away and left her.

Then she found a flight of stairs leading down. She knew they represented safety, and she breathed in a little sigh as she reached the bottom and stood looking around for the door.

She had taken a few quick steps when a bulky figure loomed at the end of a long hall—a man with shaggy hair and small, angry eyes.

Quickly she ducked into a room off the hall. Another man was lying on a sleeping bag on the floor, and she knew it was her father, although his face was hidden by shadows.

"Daddy, help me."

"I can't."

He slipped his hand under the sleeping bag, pushed at something beneath his shoulders. Then he reached toward her, called out a message she knew was important. But it was hard to make out the words.

All at once, the bad man was in the doorway. His arms lengthened, grabbed her, and she felt a choking pain as strong fingers squeezed at her windpipe, cutting off her supply of oxygen, filling her brain with swirling smoke.

Chapter Four

Swamped by terror, Marianne tried to call out for help. But no sound could get past the awful pressure of those fingers wrapped around her neck.

"The money. Give me the money," he said, over and over. "You know where it is."

A lantern loomed in the darkness. Then flames blazed up. They formed a circle around her and the man, a circle that grew smaller and smaller as orange and gold tongues licked painfully at her skin—and at his.

He shrieked—a high, frightened sound—and the choking hands slipped away from her neck. Gasping in a shuddering breath, she began to run, sobbing as she leaped through the wall of fire. But the man was right behind her, his footsteps pounding on the wooden floor, his hot breath coming in long puffs that seared her flesh as she dodged through endless dark rooms, where fire sprang from the walls.

Somewhere at the edge of her vision she saw a dark-haired boy. A boy named Nick, who had come to save her. He lunged toward her through the flames and snatched her away. It was all right. She was safe—until she realized there was a crushing weight pressing down on her chest. Panicked, she flailed out with her arms, her fists pounding against the hard wall of a man's chest.

"Marianne!" A voice penetrated the nightmare. "Marianne. Wake up. It's Tony. I won't hurt you. It's Tony."

Her eyes blinked open—and for several heartbeats she couldn't take in what was happening. All she knew was that a hard male body was pressing her into the mattress and viselike fingers had manacled her wrists.

"Baby, don't. It's all right. It's all right!"

She focused on his face, inches from hers, even as her frantic struggles subsided. He lay on top of her, his body fused to hers as his hands kept hers from beating at his head and shoulders.

When she raised her eyes to his, she found herself lost in their dark depths.

"Marianne?"

"Tony," she breathed, taking in the startling intimacy of their positions with a rush of sensation. In the next moment, she realized she'd been trying her best to pummel him. "Oh, Lord, did I hurt you?" she gasped.

"It's okay," he answered, his grip loosening on her wrists. Shifting his position, he rolled to his side.

"What…are you doing here?" she breathed.

"I heard you screaming in your sleep."

"Yes." Vivid nightmare scenes flashed in her mind. The man with his hands around her throat, choking her… The flames searing her… Suddenly she clutched at Tony's shoulders, pulling him closer, using his physical presence as a shield. "Don't leave. Don't leave me."

"I won't." Gently he cradled her body against his as she lay shaking, clinging to the one person she had always known would keep her safe.

His hands moved up and down her arms, across her back and shoulders. She closed her eyes, letting herself enjoy the sensations he aroused, feeling the fear seep out of her—but not the tension.

Her face was pressed to his naked chest. Casting her eyes down, she saw white briefs and long, hair-roughened legs.

He was practically naked in her bed. With guilty curiosity, she took a longer look and was treated to a very revealing view of white cotton knit stretched over an impressive male anatomy.

Restlessly, she shifted her legs. As they touched his, he sucked in a sharp breath, his stomach muscles tightening.

Moving quickly, he reached down, found the sheet where she had kicked it away and pulled it up so that it covered his hips and hers. Probably his intent had been modesty, but the sight of the sheet draped across the two of them, lying there like a man and a woman who had just made love was the most erotic thing she had ever seen.

"Are you okay?" he asked, his voice thick as he put a little space between their bodies.

"Sort of."

"Did you dream about the night of the fire?"

She shuddered. "Yes. But Duvalle was there. I mean the Duvalle who tried to choke me." Her hand fluttered. "It was the past and the present, all mixed up."

When she didn't volunteer any more information, he stroked her arm with his knuckles. "I need to hear about it. There might be a clue to what he wanted."

Her breath caught. She wanted to shove the evil images back into the recesses of her mind.

"How did it start?" he asked.

Hearing the urgency in his voice, she forced herself to remember. "I was in the old house. I think I was alone on the second floor."

"Yes. Your mother took you upstairs," he confirmed. "She didn't want you to see how badly your dad was wounded."

"But it's just a dream," she insisted, her temples pounding. "I mean, it's not what really happened."

"Tell me about it, anyway. Were you a little girl?"

She nodded, fighting the pain in her head as she spoke. "Yes. I saw the stairs. I went down and found my father. Then Duvalle grabbed me." She swallowed. "I mean, I guess it was him. He wouldn't let me see him yesterday."

"What did he look like in the dream?"

The image floated in her mind like the face of a spirit wavering in a crystal ball. For years she had tried to block it out. Now she deliberately opened to it. "Dark, stringy hair. Little eyes. A—a bad complexion."

Tony nodded. "That sounds like the guy I remember. Probably there's gray in his hair by now. Was he medium height and stocky?"

"Maybe, I guess. In the dream, he seemed…big."

His fingers tightened painfully on her arms. "What did he want?"

"Money," she answered as his words came back. "He said I knew where to find the money."

Tony's eyes narrowed. "What else did he say?" he demanded.

Paralysis numbed her brain. There had been more to the dream, she knew, but the images hovered at the edge of her awareness. If she concentrated, maybe she could bring them closer, into sharper focus. Yet the threat was simply too great for her to take the risk. Pain beat against the inside of her skull as her body began to shake.

She pushed at Tony. "Don't make me. Let me go!"

His hold on her gentled. "I'm sorry."

She managed a little nod. "I just can't."

He held her close, and the warmth of his body took some of the chill from her skin.

"I'd give a couple of years of my life if I could tell you what happened that night," he said grimly. "But I wasn't there."

She nodded against his chest, hearing the depths of his

anguish and knowing he didn't like this any better than she did.

She touched his cheek, and he closed his eyes. "You were in the dream," she murmured, clinging to the only part she wanted to remember. "At the end. You were trying to save me."

"Did I get to you in time?" he asked, his voice low and urgent.

"Yes." She didn't want to talk anymore, feel anymore. Like a coward, she let exhaustion overwhelm everything else. Gradually she slipped toward sleep, because this time it would be safe. This time Tony was holding her.

TONY CLOSED HIS EYES and tried to put some distance between his aching body and Marianne's. But it was impossible to hold her and ease the physical discomfort he was experiencing.

Her nightmare had brought him to her bed. But now she was asleep in his arms, and he was wrestling with his most erotic fantasy come true: Marianne snuggled up to him in bed. All he had to do was cover her mouth with his, and he could make them both forget about fires and robbers and a vengeful killer somewhere out there in the dark. But he was too damned honorable to take advantage of her—not when he'd seen the trust in her eyes and then the agony when he'd tried to force her back into the nightmare.

So he gritted his teeth and accepted the punishment for his sins. But his senses were filled with the woman next to him in bed. He could feel every inch of her long legs, her hips, the curve of her breasts. If he moved, his erection would be pressed against the juncture of her thighs. He wanted it there—wanted to bury himself in her warmth. Instead, he stayed where he was, concentrating on not waking her.

Yet he couldn't stop himself from raising his hand and

cupping his palm a fraction of an inch over her right breast where it strained against the fabric of her T-shirt. He could see the shadow of her nipple through the knit, and his fingers tingled with remembered sensations that sent the blood pounding through his body. God, she had felt so good.

And she had told Horace she was his wife.

His wife!

As he'd driven toward Paradise Beach, he'd fluctuated between anger, indignation and bemusement—and back again. He'd been prepared for anything.

And what he'd found was Marianne Leonard—playing house. Now here he was in her bed as if he had a right to make love to her. He angled his head, aching to lower his mouth to hers, to drink in her sweetness. The erotic images in his brain set his body on fire, and he had to summon every molecule of willpower he possessed to keep from thrusting his hips against hers. If he had ever needed a woman more than he needed Marianne tonight, he couldn't remember it.

But then, he'd been under her spell from the moment they'd met—when Dad and her father had initiated their strange blended family of outlaws. He had been a different person back then. An eleven-year-old without a clue to the nasty surprises life had in store for him. The first one had come one rainy morning when he woke up to find his mom had bailed out.

Then it was just him and Dad—and the little girl called Margaret and her parents. She had been four—a golden-haired angel who had snuggled up to him in the back of Dad's station wagon as they'd driven through the night and who had sneaked some of her french fries to him when her mother wasn't looking.

Life with Dad and Uncle Bobby had started out as an exciting adventure. Then he'd heard the angry, tense voices of the men and Margaret's mom, and he'd come to realize that he was on a trip to hell—and that his job was to shield Margaret from the worst of it. So he'd taken the blame for soft drinks she'd spilled and crumbs she'd left in the car, and he'd made up stories about the life they were going to live when they finally settled down. He'd spun tales about the nice brick house where she could watch Saturday-morning cartoons and play with her dog in the fenced back-yard. And he'd promised to build her a tree house and teach her to ride a skateboard.

The endless wandering had stopped abruptly. With her father dead and her mother a wreck, he'd felt even more protective of Margaret, especially when he had to watch the way she withdrew into herself. Worry had finally turned to relief when he realized that Marianne—as she was now called—didn't seem to remember the bad stuff.

Then she'd burst into adolescence, and the budding curves of her body had turned him on. He'd been ashamed of himself for getting aroused over a girl so much younger, a girl who had been like a sister, a girl who trusted him. When her mother had come over one Saturday morning to tell him to stay away from her daughter, he'd told her she had nothing to worry about. Not because she'd warned him away, but because he'd already figured out the bottom line. If he and Marianne got too close, he'd have to tell her about their fathers. And then she'd have to share the burden he'd been carrying around all these years.

She'd already made herself forget it once. Which meant that dredging up the truth would be cruel—and dangerous. What if she were too fragile to cope with the knowledge? What if it destroyed her inner peace?

For all those reasons, he'd kept Marianne Leonard at arm's length, except for small lapses like the time after his father's funeral when he'd wanted to lose himself in her.

Tonight had changed everything. When he'd heard Du-valle had come after her, had tried to strangle her, razor-sharp fear had slashed through him. He knew it was the fear of loss.

The worst part was that he'd been pushed into the role he'd always shunned. Now he was the one forcing Marianne to remember the Rossi Gang—because *her* memories could be the key to figuring out what Duvalle wanted.

TONY WOKE with a start. He hadn't expected to sleep, and his senses were immediately on alert for whatever had jerked him from slumber.

When he heard stealthy footsteps in the hall, he cursed himself for leaving the gun in the drawer beside his own bed. Damn! All he'd been thinking about when he'd come running in here was that Marianne was having a nightmare, and he had to wake her up. Things had progressed from there, and he'd forgotten all about the weapon.

As he reached for the heavy candlestick lamp on the bedside table, he heard a familiar throat-clearing sound. At the same time, Marianne gasped and snatched frantically at the sheet that had slipped below her hips.

Her movements were punctuated by a loud guffaw from the doorway. With his jaw clenched, Tony raised his head. It wasn't Duvalle blocking their exit. Instead he found himself gazing into the grinning, weathered face of Horace Haliday.

"Hi, folks," he said pleasantly, his thumbs hooked in the leather strap of his tool belt.

When he didn't get a positive response, he shuffled his booted feet. "Sorry. I knocked, but I guess you two were sleepin' too sound to hear me." He laughed.

Tony's features contorted. "What the hell are you doing sneaking in here?"

"I'm not sneaking. You left me the key. I'm supposed to be workin' on this place. Next up is the leak in the attic. *You* said you wanted it fixed before we get more rain. Your wife didn't tell me otherwise. And last night, I didn't even know if she was really your wife. Or if you'd be here in the mornin'." He ended with an elaborate shrug.

"Of course," Tony muttered. From the smug look on Horace's face, it appeared that he'd planned this scouting mission well. So much for good manners. But then, he'd always known Horace was a little odd.

"Get out of here," Tony ordered.

The intruder stayed where he was for a second, craning his neck for a better look at Marianne, who had scrunched down into the bedding. From the corner of his eye, Tony could see that her face and neck had turned beet red.

Satisfied, Horace took a step back. "Brought some groceries for you and the missus," he announced cheerfully. "A little wedding present."

Marianne gave a low moan.

"Yeah, well, my wife and I don't appreciate being accosted in our bedroom," Tony heard himself growl.

"Then you don't want me to take care of the roof this morning?" Horace asked, all innocence.

"I want you to stay away from the house until further notice. Otherwise, you're fired."

Horace looked mortally offended. "I was only doin' the job you paid me for."

Tony started to climb out of bed, reconsidered, and sat up straight, his eyes blazing. "Listen, Horace," he growled. "Mrs. Marco and I came down here to be alone. We don't want company. And we don't want a lot of people knowing we're here. So keep a lid on the gossip. You understand?"

"Sure thing." The handyman scurried off down the hall. Moments later, his heavy footsteps sounded on the stairs.

When Tony turned back to Marianne, he saw her sitting with her knees drawn up and her face cradled in her hands.

"I'm sorry," he said.

"It's my own fault," she answered, her hands still covering her face. "I should have come up with some other cover story. But I...I couldn't think."

Tony wanted to tell her how much he'd like to participate in her current cover story. He was pretty sure that was a bad idea at the moment, so he climbed out of bed and went to the window, where he could watch Horace climb back into his blue pickup truck.

Marianne shifted her legs. "We might as well get dressed."

"I'll get out of your way." He made himself scarce in his own room, but he knew to the minute when she stepped out of the shower and went downstairs. By the time he finished shaving, he could smell the aroma of sizzling country ham wafting toward him. Apparently big-hearted Horace had gone all out for the happy couple.

He hurried down the stairs, then slowed his steps as he caught sight of her rigid back.

When she said nothing, he cleared his throat. "How are you?"

She pushed the sizzling ham around in the pan and shrugged.

"I need to know."

"I'm all right."

"Good," he answered, wanting to press for more information. All right about Horace? All right about remembering the past? All right about him? The only thing he knew for sure was that she wanted him to keep his distance.

MARIANNE WANTED to turn around and shout at Tony to give her some space. But she was the one who had told Horace the story about being married, so she stayed where she was at the stove, poking needlessly at the eggs.

When he cleared his throat, she braced herself. All he said was, "I'm sorry."

About what? Duvalle's attack? Her lame excuse for com-

ing here? In her present state, she couldn't ask, so she only nodded tightly.

He remained behind her, and again the silence lengthened. "I'm sorry my prodding triggered a nightmare," he finally elaborated.

"It's happened before. I'll survive."

She heard him let out a little breath. "Will it upset you if we talk about it some more?"

"No," she made herself answer, but kept her back to him.

"You said Duvalle demanded money."

She nodded tightly. At least talking about the dream was better than talking about their screwed-up personal relationship.

"The day the Rossi Gang robbed that last bank, they got away with several hefty bags of bills from the cashiers' stations."

"The Rossi Gang. Is that what you call them?"

He gave a mirthless laugh. "Uh-huh. But I only made the mistake once of saying it to my father's face. I got a smack across the mouth."

Picturing the scene, she felt her chest tighten.

Before she could say anything, he hurried on. "What if the money is the key? What if Duvalle thinks you know where the stash is hidden?"

She whirled to face him. "I don't!"

"Maybe not on a conscious level. But you were downstairs in the room with your father. I know that much. You must have been talking to him. Or maybe you heard him and my dad making plans."

She shook her head helplessly.

"The dream could be a clue. Otherwise, I wouldn't be asking you about it."

"It was just a dream! And it was a mixture of stuff that happened a long time ago and stuff that happened yesterday. If you're planning to take it to the bank, you're crazy."

Turning back to the stove, she began furiously stirring the eggs.

She was hoping he'd disappear; instead he remained behind her, and she felt her skin prickling as she waited for him to say something else.

When she was sure she couldn't take one more mute moment, he broke the silence. "Okay. There's another possibility. My father stored a lot of papers and records here. And he was a meticulous guy. What if he wrote down something about the missing money? Maybe if I go through his stuff, I can find out something."

"You'd do that for me? Go through his stuff?" she managed to say, around the sudden lump in her throat.

"Yes."

Slowly, she turned to face him and saw a mix of warring emotions cross his features. She was certain that immersing himself in the past was the last thing he'd want to do. Yet she knew he'd made the offer for *her*.

"Thank you," she murmured.

He gave a tight nod, opened the silverware drawer, and began to clank spoons and forks onto the table.

Then, as she lifted the pan off the burner and put the ham and eggs on a platter, along with the toast she'd made, he poured coffee and opened a jar of plum preserves. They worked well together, as if they really were a couple, and she allowed herself the pleasure of focusing on the vision of cozy domesticity as she spread preserves on her toast.

Tony shattered the illusion with his next words. "What we have to do is figure out enough so we can set a trap for that scumbag Duvalle."

Chapter Five

"Set up a trap?" Marianne asked. "Why don't we just call the police?"

"Why didn't you call them when Duvalle first came after you?" Tony shot back.

She considered the question, settled for a shrug.

"Maybe you didn't remember your father's criminal career. But on a gut level, you knew that calling the cops was a bad idea," he said. "Now you understand that explaining your background could be a problem. What if the *police* think the same thing as Duvalle—that you know where to find the stolen money?"

She bit back a sharp answer and pushed her eggs around the plate. Tony was trying to come up with a solution to their problem. What's more, he was trying to act as if nothing embarrassing had happened this morning.

But she was having trouble coping with something as simple as sitting across from him.

"I can go into town and pick up some things I need while you're looking through your father's stuff," she ventured.

"No." The answer was instantaneous and decisive.

She raised her eyes in surprise. "Why not?"

"Too dangerous. The fewer people who know you're in town, the better."

Despite the morning heat, she felt a shiver sweep over

her skin. "You don't think Duvalle is going to show up at Paradise Beach, do you?"

"I hope not. But I'm not going to take any chances. If you need anything from the store, I'll get it."

She thought about the things she wanted to buy. Clean underwear. Deodorant. Other personal items. Sending Tony with that kind of shopping list was out of the question.

"I—I guess I'll just wash some stuff," she murmured as she rose and carried her plate to the counter. Setting it down, she began to run water in the pan.

Behind her, she heard his chair scrape back. "Then I'll start on the research project."

She nodded, waiting to hear his retreating footsteps before turning around. Like her, he'd hardly touched his breakfast—a pretty good sign that he wasn't quite so calm, cool and collected as he pretended.

SHE HAD INTENDED to stay out of his way for the rest of the morning. But her plans had changed on her way back from washing her underwear and sticking it in the dryer. When she spotted the telephone, she stopped short. She was supposed to be at work today, and her boss was bound to be worried if she didn't call in.

Hesitantly, she tapped on the closed study door.

"Yes?" Tony called out.

She pushed open the door but didn't move into the room. He was sitting on the leather couch, cardboard boxes spread around him on the free cushions and the floor.

"Is it safe to use the phone here?" she asked.

"For what?"

"I forgot about the Light Street Foundation. I should call them. They're probably wondering what happened to me."

His face turned thoughtful. "Tell them you had a sudden emergency—with a sick friend. If they ask for the number, say you don't know it, and you'll get back to them."

She hesitated. "I don't like lying to them."

"I know, but it's necessary. Suppose when Duvalle can't find you, he starts nosing around your building. If they know where you are, he might find out."

She shuddered, silently admitting he was right. "How long am I going to be away with this sick friend?" she asked, her voice tight.

He shrugged. "A few days."

"I can't just take an unscheduled leave of absence. They need me."

"When we're in a position to explain, we will," he said with forced patience.

She didn't like the solution. But she couldn't think of anything better. So she dialed Erin Stone, her boss, aware that Tony was watching and listening.

"Marianne, are you all right?" Erin asked as soon as she picked up the phone.

"Yes. But something…unexpected came up."

There was a pause on the other end of the line. "Can we help?"

"I don't think so."

"Marianne, we're equipped to deal with all kinds of emergencies."

"Yes. Thanks. I—I'll call you if I can't make it back to the office in a couple of days."

She hung up as soon as she could, and raised her eyes to Tony. "Was that okay?"

"Fine. I know that was hard for you."

"Yes." She was about to turn and stride down the hall. But the brief exchange had convinced her that ignoring the tension between them wasn't doing either of them any good.

"Tony, we have to talk," she said.

"About what?"

"Us."

"Not now." He picked up one of the boxes and began shuffling through the papers. "I want to get this over with."

"I know," she answered. "But I need to say some things before we both blow our tops."

"Care to explain that last remark?" He raised his head, his eyes narrowed.

Any other time, the pose and the look in his eye would have been enough to stop her. Not today. With false steadiness, she plunged ahead. "Being thrown together like this is hard for both of us. Because we're both worried about Duvalle showing up. But that's not all of it." She stopped, swallowed. "We've been forced into a...a kind of relationship that makes us both uncomfortable. It's partly my fault, for making up that stupid story about being your wife."

"Forget it. We'll survive."

Too wound up to quit, she plowed ahead. "I used to wonder why you stopped being my friend when I grew up."

"I never stopped being your friend!"

"Okay. Maybe I mean I never understood why you acted like I was the most unattractive girl you'd ever seen. Now I get it. I'm from a part of your life that you hate—a past you wish you could forget."

The way his body jerked back told her she was correct. "But the Rossi Gang is out in the open now. And maybe there was one good thing that came out of what our fathers did." Gulping in a breath, she held it until her lungs began to burn, then blurted, "Maybe that good thing is us. Our fathers brought us together. And we got close to each other. We were like a family, only the bond was even stronger because of what we went through. After we moved to Baltimore, you cared enough to protect me from the past. But you don't have to do that anymore. We're both grown up, and we don't have to pretend anything."

When he didn't speak, she surged on. "I mean it's crazy to keep pretending like we're not drawn to each other.

We're not kids. We're a man and a woman, and it's obvious we both want to…to explore a relationship.''

She was dizzy with amazement that she'd dared to say so much. For years she'd wanted to tell him what was in her heart. Now it was out in the open.

She felt as if she were poised on a balance beam and could fall off either side. But would Tony be there to catch her? He didn't move, and she was suddenly sure that she'd gone too far. Or maybe she was dead wrong. Maybe his feelings for her were nothing like her feelings for him. In that case, she'd just made an utter and complete fool of herself.

Her only consolation was that she hadn't given everything away. She hadn't told him that she loved him and that the idea of pretending to be his wife must have come from some deep subconscious wish.

Head bowed, she spun away and hurried upstairs to the room where she'd slept. The sight of the unmade bed brought a blush to her cheeks as she remembered the way they'd woken up.

Quickly she straightened the sheets, plumped the pillows and did her best to erase the memories of the night.

TONY CLOSED the office door and leaned back against the wooden barrier. He still couldn't believe the things Marianne had said a few minutes ago. It seemed she could read him like a book. Still, if she knew how much he wanted to pull her into his arms and devour her, she'd be shaking in her sandals.

God, he wanted her. But in his mind, he'd always known that making love with her would mean making a commitment, and he didn't know if either one of them was ready for that—given the pressure cooker they were in. Not only were they dealing with the Rossi Gang, but their awareness of each other was on overload.

Pushing himself away from the door, he rubbed his damp palms against his jeans, unable to keep from thinking about the feel of her flesh under his hands. He'd taken advantage of every excuse to touch her.

And he'd better start thinking about something else—like Arlan Duvalle, for instance. He sighed. The way things were shaping up, it looked like he couldn't keep Marianne safe here and also go after the sicko. Much as he hated to admit it, he needed help. And that meant laying out the whole situation to someone else.

He clenched his teeth, then forced his jaw to relax and reached for the phone. Ironically, he was planning to call to the same building Marianne had phoned a few minutes ago.

Instead of dialing the number of the Light Street Foundation, however, he called private detective Mike Lancer, who had done some work for him in the past when he'd needed background checks on potential business associates. He was a good guy. Discreet. And very efficient.

SLIPPING QUIETLY down the stairs again, Marianne was relieved not to bump into Tony. If she was lucky, maybe he'd stay out of her way for the rest of the day. She retrieved her laundry and put her underwear back on. Feeling a little less vulnerable, she eased out the front door and flopped onto the porch glider, hoping she could save Tony from his self-appointed task by remembering some more details from the night of the fire. But after half an hour, she silently admitted that she was wasting her time trying to dredge up memories buried so deep in her subconscious that they fought to the surface only in nightmares.

Maybe on some hidden level she'd always known what was going on. Maybe she'd been a participant in the conspiracy of silence. Her mother. Uncle Silvio. Tony. They'd all kept the truth from her, and she'd let them do it. She'd never questioned the blank place in her memory because she'd sensed it might destroy her.

Clasping her knees, she rocked back and forth, thinking of all the lies she'd gladly accepted from her mother. Finally, too miserable to sit still, she stood and began to pace along the porch. Soon, the small space was too confining, and the sun slanting under the roof was too hot. Tiptoeing down the hall, she made a pitcher of iced tea and gulped a glass while she scribbled Tony a note telling him she'd be down at the dock.

A stiff breeze was blowing off the water as she reached the dock, and she lifted her hair, letting the wind dry the perspiration on her neck. Grateful for the slight relief from the heat, she stepped onto the worn boards and scanned the horizon. Dark clouds were gathering in the sky to the west, heralding a thunderstorm. Good. Maybe it would drive away some of the stifling air—and clear her head so she could think.

But it was no easier to concentrate out here, she discovered after yet another session of trying to force her mind past the old barrier. Apparently, on some deep level of self-preservation, she didn't want to know what had happened that night. All she could do was bring up images of a dark-haired boy who looked a lot like Tony.

Her eyes focused on the choppy water. Just as a tern swooped below the surface, she heard a noise behind her. Going very still, she listened intently, and the sound resolved itself into footsteps crunching along the gravel path.

Trapped! She should never have come out here—not to such an isolated place. Heart thumping inside her chest, she eyed the water, estimating her chances of getting away, then spared a frantic glance over her shoulder.

It was Tony, not Duvalle, and she felt her tension ease down several notches. Still, she realized that until the stalker was in custody again, she would always feel as if she were being followed.

He halted about two feet away on the narrow pier, the muscles in his arms clenching and unclenching as he squeezed his hand into a fist and loosened it again.

The wind picked up, filling the silence with its moaning voice, and she felt her nerves begin to snap. What had he discovered? All she knew was that it must be something bad. Yet he'd come to her.

"Tony?"

Seconds ticked by and she blurted, "Did you find out the fire was my fault?" she blurted.

"What?"

"The fire. Was it my fault?"

"Not the fire," he muttered, scuffing his foot against the worn boards. Something about the sound tore at her, and she pivoted. One quick glance at the desolation she saw etched into his stark features was enough to wedge an instant lump in her throat.

"Tony, what's wrong?"

He swiped a hand through his hair. "My dad and I didn't exactly get along," he muttered.

"Yes," she answered softly. That was nothing new.

"You told Duvalle a story about your father writing you a letter. Well, mine actually did. It was right at the top of one of the boxes." He took a crumpled piece of paper from his pocket, started to unfold it, then changed his mind and shoved it back. The look on his face was as stormy as the clouds gathering around them.

Taking two small steps forward, she put her hands on his shoulders. "What he wrote—is it something bad?" she murmured. "Something about the old days that he couldn't admit to you?"

Tony's jaw was rigid. "He said that he knew how I felt about his criminal career. He said that if I'd come looking through his things and found the letter, I must have forgiven him for the mistakes he made.'' He stopped abruptly, looking like a small boy who had lost his way in a swamp. "Too bad he didn't know why I ended up poking in his boxes of stuff.''

"Oh, Tony.''

The color had drained from his face. "When he was alive, we never had a decent conversation about his former life. All this time I was making assumptions—and they were wrong.''

He pulled the letter from his pocket again and held it out to her.

When she stared at him helplessly, he folded it into her hand. "Read it.''

She shouldn't invade his privacy. Yet he obviously wanted her to know what his father had said.

Slowly she unfolded the paper, smoothed out the wrinkles and began to read the bold, slanting handwriting.

"Dear Son,
     I made a lot of mistakes in my life. The worst one was letting my friend Bobby St. Paul talk me into a career of robbery.''

She raised her eyes to Tony. "It was my father's idea?''
He gave a tight nod, but said nothing. Shaken, she dropped her gaze to the letter again, blinking to clear her vision.

"I'm not making excuses for myself. For a while, our life of crime was pretty exciting. We felt like we were beating the system. But then I realized I was tearing my family apart. Your mother walked away, and that left you and me. I needed you to be strong and steady, and you were. For me. For Margaret and her mother. I know I loaded you up with more than any kid should have to carry on his shoulders—while we were on the road and after we moved to Baltimore.

"Hooking up with Arlan Duvalle was our biggest mistake. And you know how the whole thing ended. I will never get over Bobby's death and never be able to make that up to Marianne and her mother—although I've tried my best.

"I bought them new identities. I've helped support them. I've been there for Marianne, and I hope I've made up at least in part for the loss of her father.

"I did other things, too, to make amends—like giving away a lot of the money we stole to charity and to the church. I know you think I bought the summer house at Paradise Beach with stolen money. That's only partly true. I made some good investments—and used the windfall to buy the property. I kept it over the years in case we ever needed a place to disappear.

"I know I've been hard on you—harder than a father should be. Probably you've guessed that I didn't want you to turn out like me. I will always feel guilty for taking away your childhood. But if you are reading this letter now, that means you feel good enough about our relationship to go through my papers. And perhaps you have even forgiven me for my past sins.

"You know I was never good at saying what I should to you. But I'm proud of you, son. I'm proud of the life you've made for yourself. And I hope you can find peace and happiness.

Love,
Dad"

Her eyes were wet by the time she finished reading. "Oh, Tony," she breathed.

"Why couldn't he *tell* me any of that?" he grated.

"Because he was a lot like you," she answered. "He had strong feelings about…about the people he loved. But he was afraid to let himself express them," she added softly, blinking back the moisture in her eyes.

"One thing I learned from him is that feelings are painful," he answered, the wind whipping at his raw voice.

"Not always, Tony." Gambling everything on one roll of the dice, she reached upward and took him in her arms, her eyes locking with his. They darkened to onyx pools as she wrapped him close, offering him whatever he was willing to take from her.

Chapter Six

For heartbeats he held himself rigid, and she thought she had lost the gamble. Then a dam seemed to burst inside him, and he moved with sudden speed, dragging her into the prison of his arms as his lips came down on hers.

"Marianne." Her name sighed out of him, like a plea—a culmination of the feelings building between them since he'd first hauled her out of the water.

Finally she felt all the heat, all the desperation he had been hiding with such determination. With a little cry, she gave herself up to both.

He answered with a muted growl that welled from deep in his chest as his mouth traveled over hers, tasting, devouring, demanding.

Sensations burst within her—all the sensations she'd been struggling to contain. Now she was helpless to stop the rush of feelings—physical and emotional—that claimed her.

He needed her! At least for this moment in time, and she gloried in the knowledge.

So many nights alone in bed, she had longed for his kiss. She hadn't imagined the potency of his mouth melding with hers. All she could do was cling to this man she had loved for so long, letting him teach her with his lips and tongue and teeth how erotic a simple thing like a kiss could be.

As she clung to him, she was dimly aware of the wind

whipping around them and the waves dashing against the pilings. But the gathering storm was far less powerful than the reality of Tony's mouth tasting and teasing her and his arms clasping her heated body against his.

The air had grown chilled, magnifying the warmth of his hands as they slid beneath the hem of her T-shirt, the imprint of his fingers burning into the flesh of her back.

When he shifted her so that he could cup her breasts and stroke his fingers across the aching tips, she felt herself moan her pleasure into his mouth.

His hands went around her hips then, dragging her against him—letting her feel the hard shaft of his arousal. Mindlessly, she moved against him. Just as he began to move with her, a bolt of lightning arced in a jagged line across the sky, followed by a hollow clap of thunder that boomed over the water and shook the pier.

His head jerked up and he looked around, taking in the sudden darkness.

"We can't stay here. Come on."

Disappointment jolted through her as the warmth of his body detached itself from hers. Taking her hand, he started toward the house, his pace increasing when another thunderclap reverberated around them and a few large drops of water began to spatter onto the pier.

She stumbled after him, disoriented and disappointed. Of all the damn bad luck.

ARLAN DUVALLE SAT at a booth in the Dirty Duck Bar and Lounge, his large hands wrapped around a mug of beer to keep them from shaking. He'd come into this local hangout by chance, just to get out of the rain. When the bartender had eyed him pointedly, he'd ordered a beer and a crab-cake dinner. He'd soon found that listening to the locals chatter was very instructive. The most interesting topic of conversation was between a couple of old goats named Horace and Frank. It seemed Horace had stumbled onto something pretty juicy—Tony Marco and his new bride. Apparently the new Mrs. Marco had shown up last night—by herself. Marianne was her name. Tony had come down later.

Arlan clenched his hands on the beer mug, thinking about blind luck and modern technology. After running into a dead end in Baltimore, he'd done a quick computer check of Marianne Leonard's credit-card purchases and found she'd purchased a tank of gas at a station on the outskirts of Paradise Beach.

He figured she'd taken off randomly for some beach town, and he'd sped down here hoping she was still in the area. Within minutes of walking into the Dirty Duck, he'd come to find she was holed up with Tony Marco at an estate his dad had undoubtedly purchased with his ill-gotten gains.

Arlan suppressed a chuckle. He'd been in the dark about the estate, but now he was in the driver's seat again. Taking a couple of sips of beer, he thought about making a phone call to the lovebirds, surprising them with another one of his faultless imitations.

But he resisted the temptation. If he tipped them off that something was up, they might fly the coop. Instead, he'd wait until the rain stopped. Then he'd see about arranging a nice surprise for them.

He rolled his mug between his palms, thinking of interesting possibilities. One idea took his fancy, and he tipped back his head, downing the rest of his brew.

He'd have to buy some stuff. But that was no big deal. With the money he'd stashed while he was in prison he could get what he wanted at that new shopping center down the road. After throwing a couple of bills on the table, he slipped out of the booth and ambled toward his car.

A BARRAGE of fat raindrops caught them just short of the porch. Grabbing Marianne's hand, Tony pulled her under the shelter, then opened the front door.

When he made no move to go in, she laid a hand on his arm.

"I'm sorry," he said.

"About what?"

"Taking liberties."

She raised her head, forced herself to meet his gaze. Along with apology, she saw something dark and dangerous smoldering in the depths of his eyes.

"You weren't taking liberties," she said.

"What do you call it?" he tossed back.

She pressed her hands to her sides to keep them from trembling, amazed that she was still standing here arguing. Swallowing his rejection and walking away had become a habit. But this time she would fight for what she wanted—what he wanted, too, if he'd simply admit it.

"I think I already told you. I call it giving the two of us a chance. Not backing away because you think it's the honorable thing to do. Or because you're in the habit of protecting me from the Rossi Gang." She took a step toward him, then another so that she was almost as close as she'd been on the pier.

He didn't move back.

"Before the storm interrupted us, was I pushing you into something you didn't want to do?" she asked.

"No."

"Good," she finished the word with her lips lightly resting against his and her heart slamming against the inside of her chest. If he pulled away from her now, something inside her would die.

But he didn't pull away. Instead, his arms came up to imprison her, and his head angled to take her mouth in a hot, savage kiss.

She made a small sound that was part triumph, part surrender as his lips moved against hers—rekindling the fierce heat that had leaped between them on the dock. When he finally broke the contact, they were both breathing hard, both swaying on their feet.

"Come up to the bedroom," she murmured, the invitation punctuated by another jolt of lightning. Talk about symbolism!

"Marianne. You're not thinking straight. We can't just make love. I don't have any way to protect you."

"Uh…I think you do."

His eyebrows lifted.

She felt her cheeks flame. But she plowed ahead. "When I, ah, went to look for a shirt in your drawer I found a box of condoms."

She heard him mutter a low oath. Before he could elaborate, she grabbed his hand and bolted for the stairs. He stayed right behind her, making her both exalted and nervous with her victory. She wanted this. She had wanted this for a long time. But now that the moment had come, she was feeling suddenly shy as she pulled open the dresser drawer, retrieved the box she'd seen and set it on the bedside table.

Still with her back to him, she pulled her T-shirt over her head with a jerky motion and tossed it onto the chair. Her shorts followed. Clad in her underwear, she was pulling back the covers when his hand on her arm stopped her.

"Marianne?"

"Come to bed with me," she answered, without turning, fighting to keep her voice steady and her heart from pounding its way through her chest wall.

"Not when you're wound as tight as a mainspring. Why are you doing this? Are you thinking that you owe me something for trying to help you out of the mess with Duvalle?"

"Of course not! Are you still looking for excuses to back out?"

"I'm trying to figure out what's going on here. You're acting like a sacrificial virgin."

"I am not!"

Gently he turned her to face him. "Marianne?"

Her lower lip trembled. Stepping forward, she pressed her face against his shoulder. "Okay, I'm afraid that when you find out I don't have a lot of experience, you'll...stop." That was the truth—or part of it. The rest had to do with her own uncertainties.

With a hand under her chin, he tipped her face up toward his. "How much experience are we talking about?" he asked quietly.

She swallowed hard. Better get it over with. "Tony, when I thought about making love for the first time, it was always with you. I haven't accepted any substitutes."

He swore under his breath.

"Some guys would be pleased," she whispered, daring to trail her fingers across the front of his T-shirt, feeling the muscles in his broad chest quiver under her touch.

"Some guys would be worried about doing it right."

"Are you?"

"Yeah."

She gave a nervous little laugh. "At least you know I'm not going to be making comparisons."

When he didn't speak, her hand stilled, but she forced herself to say, "If you don't want me, I guess you'd better leave."

"I want you, all right." His arms enveloped her, folded her possessively to him, and she let out the breath she'd been holding. This time his kiss was gentler, softer. But that wasn't what she wanted. She wanted to feel his hunger, to feel the power flow between them again. Wordlessly, she moved her mouth against his, telling him she would take as much of him—body and soul—as he was willing to give her.

TONY WATCHED her face as he unhooked her bra, and tossed it out of the way, letting her know that things were on the verge of getting very serious. The combination of trust and nervousness he saw warring in her eyes threatened to swamp him.

All the more reason he owed her one last chance to change her mind. So he stayed planted where he was, admiring the view. She was gorgeous, her breasts rounded and high, the nipples already tightly budded for him. The sight of her made his own body tighten painfully.

She gave him a cocky smile that told him she knew exactly why he was standing there, looking but not touching. Closing the distance between them, she reached for the hem of his shirt, tugged it up, and pulled it over his head, just as another jagged flash of lightning split the sky.

Of course, she spoiled the bold effect by taking her lower lip between her teeth.

He stopped thinking about effects when she trailed her fingers over the old burn scars, then clasped her arms around him, drawing his chest to hers, naked flesh to naked flesh. A tremor of primitive desire shuddered through his body as he felt the sweet pressure of her breasts.

"Marianne…" he gasped, forgetting all the reasons he'd sworn he'd never hold her like this.

"Umm," she answered, her voice dreamy, heavy with promise as his fingers trailed up and down her back, lingering on her silky skin.

Shifting her in his arms, he rubbed his chest against her breasts. The sensation was so exquisite that his knees went weak. Hers too, it seemed, as he felt her sway on unsteady legs.

He anchored her with one arm, the other hand drifting up and down her spine as he rained tiny kisses along her cheek, down to her ear, and along her jaw.

She tasted wonderful. Bending lower, he found one distended nipple and swirled his tongue around it.

"Oh!" she breathed, then "oh," again as he took it into his mouth and sucked.

She clung to him, a tiny sob welling in her throat as his lips drew on her sweetness while his free hand found her other breast.

The depth of her response made him dizzy. Almost frantic with the need to possess every inch of her, he slid his hands under the waistband of her panties, stroking over her sweetly rounded bottom before slipping the wisp of lace down her legs.

"Okay?" he asked as he felt her tense.

"Yes," she answered against his chest.

Once again, he tipped her face toward his. "Don't hide from me, baby."

He saw her swallow. "I've never been naked with a man. It makes me feel kind of…exposed."

"It should make you feel beautiful. I never knew how beautiful until now."

She flushed, the color spreading across her chest, down to the tops of her breasts.

"So let's try it from a different angle." Scooping her up, he laid her on the bed, then stripped off his slacks. He left his briefs on, hoping the barrier of knit fabric would remind him to take this slow and easy. Then he lay down beside her and gathered her to him.

Still sensing the combination of arousal and tension in her, he kissed her cheek, stroked her shoulders, then turned on his back, taking her with him so that the length of her body was draped over his and his arms circled her shoulders.

"What are we doing?" she asked, her voice hitching.

"Hugging."

She gave him a low laugh. "I've never been hugged quite like this."

"Good."

Outside, rain drummed on the roof, but the storm was only a dull background noise. All his senses were focused on the woman above him.

Reaching for her mouth with his, he kissed her hungrily as his hands molded to her, stroking over her shoulders, down her hips, pressing her against him.

"Tony," she moaned, her body moving on its own, sliding over his with an erotic rhythm as old as time. Desire shot through him, and he ached to reverse their positions and bury himself in her warmth. But he kept her where she was, touching her, kissing her, as they pushed each other toward a place where there was only hot sensation, burning need.

When she lifted her head and looked down at him, her breathing was ragged and her eyes were deep, limpid pools.

"I think if you hug me any more, I'm going to...to..."

"Detonate?" he inquired thickly, describing his own desperate state.

She nodded gravely.

He eased her to her back. "Beautiful," he murmured, as his hand drifted over her, down to her abdomen...and lower.

When he took a gliding stroke and then another through her most intimate flesh, she arched into the caress, instinctively seeking more.

"And so sexy."

She was slick and wet, utterly his—and yet so vulnerable that his chest tightened to the point of pain.

"Oh, Tony. This is so good. So good."

"Yes," he answered, hearing the thickness in his own voice.

"Show me the next part."

His hand was shaking as he stripped off his briefs and found the box of condoms on the bedside table. When he turned back to her, she held out her arms to him.

His virgin bride, he thought, dazed by the notion. "I don't want to hurt you," he said as he moved between her legs.

"It doesn't matter. Nothing matters but loving you. Now. Please, now."

Her hands went around him, urging him to her, and he made the decision that a swift possession would cause her the least pain. Still, her sharp gasp as he breached the barrier tore at his soul.

"Are you all right?" he questioned urgently.

She managed a tight nod. But when he started to pull back, she held him firmly to her.

"Marianne—"

"Love me."

All he could do was obey, moving slowly at first, then faster as he felt her body ease into the unfamiliar rhythm.

She climbed with him in a spiral of demand until she was digging her nails into his shoulders, her little cries and the frantic movement of her hips driving him toward the point of no return.

"I…Tony…I need…"

He slid his hand between them, stroked her as his body moved within her. Exaltation flooded through him when he felt her inner muscles clench. As she sobbed out his name, he followed her over the edge into ecstasy.

MARIANNE FLOATED back to earth—or rather to the bed where Tony held her in his arms. She stroked her lips against his neck, longing to say the words swelling her heart. She loved him, and ached to hear the same confession from him. But he didn't say it, and she told herself she'd known that making love wasn't going to mean a commitment, even if this was—kind of—their wedding night. So she simply held on to him, to the joy he'd given her.

"How are you?" he asked, his lips playing with her ear.

"Good," she answered, fighting fatigue, her words slurring a little. "Very...very good."

He smiled down at her, then tenderly smoothed back a lock of her damp hair. "You didn't get much sleep last night. Close your eyes."

She watched him pull the sheet up and settle it around their waists. Like last night. Only this was the real thing, she thought with a satisfied smile. She wanted to stay awake, to savor the aftermath of making love, but between her fatigue and the drumming of raindrops on the roof, she found it impossible to keep her lids open.

Chapter Seven

Marianne woke to darkness and the smell of smoke. It seemed to wrap around her, choke off her breath like the hands of Arlan Duvalle wrapped around her neck.

Smoke. Fire.

Jagged claws of primal fear tore at her. With a muffled cry, she rolled toward Tony, her fingers digging into his shoulders. He came awake, blinking at her in the darkness.

"What?"

"Fire!" she gasped, her voice high and urgent.

"Your dream," he murmured, as he reached for her hand.

"No." She fought against him, against the seductive comfort of his embrace. Fire had been her nightmare for years, and now it was all coming true again.

"Can't you smell it?" She struggled to keep her voice below the level of hysteria.

He drew in a breath, his body stiffening as he caught the acrid scent. Then the sound of a chair toppling to the wood floor made them both go still.

Seconds later, Tony's feet were on the floor and his hands were fumbling for the clothing he'd discarded. "The bastard's found us!" he growled as he pulled on his jeans.

Panic rising like a flood tide in her brain, she whirled toward the door, suppressing a cough as a wave of smoke hit her. If they didn't get out of here right now, it was going to be too late.

Tony pushed the door closed, blocking off the smoke, and held her tight as she struggled to get free. "Wait. Not that way." He was already sliding open the drawer of the bedside table and pulling out the gun she'd seen last night.

As her gaze darted from the door to the weapon, he moved his mouth close to her ear again. "Somehow he figured out we're here. He filled the place with smoke, and he's waiting for you to come stumbling down the stairs. So you go out the window like you did at your house. Meet me at the car."

"What are you going to do?" she hissed.

"Go down there and get the bastard," he said as he handed her the shorts and shirt she'd discarded on the floor.

Every nerve in her body vibrated as she held fast to his arm. "No!"

His voice turned fierce, giving her no choice. "I'm not taking any chances with you. Get moving. And if—"

"If what?"

"If I run into trouble, go for help."

She stood there, almost too numb to react. The smoke from below had seeped into her brain like poison, making it almost impossible to think. When Tony gave her a push toward the window, she let him make the decision for her.

For the second time in two days, she climbed onto a porch roof. But she didn't know *this* porch, didn't know the location of the downspout—if there was one.

After the rain, the old shingles were slippery, and she had to move cautiously to keep her balance as she picked her way on all fours toward a large tree with overhanging limbs.

Halfway there, her foot slipped and she went down on her elbows. A gasp welled in her throat as she slid toward the roof edge, scraping herself against the rough surface as she fought for purchase. Frantically, she reached over her head, scrabbled for one of the branches and managed to stop herself from tumbling to the ground.

Then, willing her heart to stop thumping, she eased her body cautiously onto the limb, inching outward until she was clear of the porch. About six feet from the ground, she jumped the rest of the way, flexing her legs to break her fall. Swaying, she steadied herself against the tree trunk, her gaze trained on the house. Inside she could hear someone coughing and flinched from the sound.

Tony had ordered her to run for the car—to go for help. And every cell in her brain screamed for her to get away— to escape from the smoke and the fire.

Then shots cracked in the darkness, and she went stockstill. She wanted to shout to Tony, to make sure he was all right. But that would only put him in worse danger—and tell Duvalle she was outside.

Crouching low, she started for the back door, expecting at any moment to see the window erupt in flames. An angry roar from Duvalle stopped her in midstride. The exclamation was followed by the sound of splintering wood. Pounding forward, she looked wildly around for a weapon and spotted the shovel that Horace Haliday must have left leaning against the house.

Snatching it up, she leaped for the door. When she flung it open, smoke billowed out in a choking wave. The thought that Tony was inside kept her from running headlong into the night. Instead she dragged in a gulping draft of air and stepped into the kitchen.

Immediately her eyes stung and her lungs burned. But she pushed forward, and the sound of thrashing and crashing led her to the living room. Through the thick smoke, she made out the coffee table lying in pieces and two figures rolling on the rug, locked in deadly combat. There was no problem telling the men apart, since Duvalle must have outweighed Tony by fifty pounds.

At the moment, the intruder was on top. Before they could trade positions, Marianne brought the blade of the shovel down on his meaty shoulder.

Duvalle screamed, and Tony lifted him in the choking air, sending him crashing to the floor in front of the ruined coffee table where he sprawled—inert.

But the effort had taken every bit of Tony's strength, and he staggered back, hit the wall and slid to the floor, coughing.

"Tony! Tony, are you all right?" she shouted, leaping toward him.

His eyes were closed, and his breath had turned shallow. As she bent over him, scrambling sounds came from the other side of the room. Whirling, she made out Duvalle, who had pushed himself up and stood swaying on his feet like a ghost in the mist. But he was no ghost. She could smell the stale odor of his sweat through the fumes that clogged the room.

Moving to the back of the sofa, he snatched a smoking bucket from the floor and hurled it at them. Marianne screamed and ducked. But the missile only made it to the area rug.

With a curse, Duvalle turned and staggered away as the bucket rolled back and forth, sending charred wood and paper spewing out. Her heart in her throat, Marianne watched as small fires flared up and began to eat away at the rug's fibers.

If she'd been alone, nothing would have kept her in the house. But Tony was still sprawled against the wall only a few yards away.

Teeth clenched to keep from screaming, she leaped forward and grabbed the corner of the rug. Fear took on a new meaning as heat seared her hand. But she didn't let go. Instead, with a moan, she folded the heavy fabric over itself to smother the flames.

Choking, she tugged the burning mass toward the window. She was sure the whole thing was about to go up in her face, but somehow she managed to hang on long enough to pitch it through the window where it landed in a heap and flared briefly before the soggy ground dampened the fire.

Panting, coughing, she turned back to Tony. He had pushed himself to a sitting position and was gazing at her in a kind of stunned wonder. All she could do was stand there swaying.

He tried to move and groaned. The sound snapped her out of her trance. "Are you all right?" she gasped, dropping to his side.

"Yeah." He stared up at her in amazement. "That was the bravest thing I ever saw."

She shook her head. It hadn't been a matter of bravery, but of necessity.

"You were unconscious," she whispered. "I had to."

"You should have gotten the hell out of here."

"I couldn't leave you."

She saw him swallow, felt his fingers fumble for hers and squeeze. "Thank you."

"Thank you for coming down here when you knew Duvalle was trying to smoke us out."

He gave a little nod, then raised his head. "Where is he?"

"He threw the burning bucket at us and disappeared. But we'd better get out of here in case he comes back."

Tony moved with painful slowness as he pushed himself to a standing position, using a chair for support.

When she reached for his arm, he made a strangled sound, and she realized suddenly that his flesh was wet and sticky, with a trail of blood dripping down to his hand.

"Tony?"

"It's nothing," he muttered, swaying on his feet.

She bent to take a better look at the arm. "He shot you!"

"It's not so bad." Gritting his teeth, he started toward the kitchen. When he listed to his right, she hurried to steady him.

He stopped by a counter, opened a drawer, and pulled out a clean dish towel. Turning on a light, he inspected his mangled arm. Then he handed her the towel. "Wrap it around the wound and tie it tight," he ordered.

"You need a doctor."

"It can wait. It's a flesh wound, as they say in the cowboy movies. Just patch me up, ma'am."

She wound the makeshift bandage round his arm, biting her lips when he couldn't hold back a swiftly indrawn breath.

Blood soaked immediately through the cloth.

"Tony—"

"I'm fine! I want you out of here. Before he changes his mind and comes back to finish what he started."

Turning away, he eyed the phone, then shrugged and stepped briskly onto the porch. When he missed the first stair, he cursed sharply as he grabbed the railing to keep from pitching forward.

She followed behind, ready to pick him up if he blacked out. However, she wasn't entirely surprised that he made it to the car on his own. If Tony Marco was anything, he was tough.

After easing onto the seat, he dug into his pocket and fished out his keys, handing them across the console.

As she stared down at them, a thought struck her. "My purse—"

"We'll get it later."

"What if a cop wants to see my license?"

"Drive carefully."

"Right," she answered, feeling strangely light-headed. Leaning over Tony, she touched his face. His skin was cold, and moisture beaded his skin, giving her the sudden memory of another wounded man. Her father. He'd been shot, too. When she made a strangled noise, Tony pressed his fingers over hers.

"I'll be okay. Just get us out of here."

Throwing the car into gear, she eased forward, her headlights cutting through the gloom as she swung around toward the access road. When she hit the highway, she hesitated. "Where are we going?"

"Baltimore," he replied, his voice barely audible, his eyes closed.

"We should stop at the nearest hospital."

"No!" he growled, so she simply kept driving through the darkness.

He sat with his eyes closed and his head thrown back, breathing shallowly as she drove toward the city, glancing at him every few minutes. He looked like he was asleep—or passed out.

Her eyes flicked to the gas gauge. The tank was half-full, thank goodness, so they wouldn't have to stop.

An image of herself pumping gas stole into her mind, and her foot bounced on the accelerator. She had stopped to get gas outside Paradise Beach—and she'd been dumb enough to pay with a credit card. Was that how Duvalle had found them?

She wanted to confess her mistake to Tony, but bothering him now was out of the question. So she kept driving into the darkness, her hands fused to the wheel, her thoughts swirling in her head. Duvalle had known she was afraid of fire, and he'd used that knowledge against her tonight. But maybe it wasn't just the flames and smoke that terrified her. On the pier, she'd blurted out a question: *Did he say the fire was my fault?*

She stared ahead, her gaze fixed on the taillights of the car in front of her. Had she started the fire? Was that why she'd blocked that night out of her memory?

At the I-95 on-ramp, Tony startled her by speaking. "Take me...to Miguel Valero. You...know where...he lives?"

"Yes."

Turning off the highway, she headed for a neighborhood at the fringes of Fells Point, where the Valeros had recently moved. Like Marianne, Jessie, Miguel's wife, was a social worker at the Light Street Foundation. She'd been doing some of her work at home since their son, Michael, had been born seven months ago, and Marianne had brought her files from time to time.

She found the house, pulled up at the curb, and looked at her watch, amazed to find that it was only around ten in the evening. Somehow, she'd thought it was the middle of the night. Apparently Duvalle had made his move just after dark.

Miguel, who had opened a medical clinic not far from the house, answered her knock at the door.

"Were you in a fire?" he asked as soon as he caught a whiff of their clothing.

"Yes. We're not burned, but Tony's been shot."

"Then drive the car around back and we'll get him inside," he answered without missing a beat.

Miguel helped Tony into a small medical office in the walkout basement. As he eased him onto the examination table, Jessie drew Marianne into the waiting room.

"Sit down," she said. "Do you want something to drink? Water? A soda? Something stronger?"

"I'm fine." Marianne answered, sinking onto an imitation-leather couch and glancing toward the exam room. Miguel was blocking her view of Tony.

"Well, you may not be thirsty, but you're not fine. What happened?" her friend asked. "I know you called this morning and said you wouldn't be at work."

Her mind spun back to the phone conversation. She'd

been evasive with Erin earlier, but this was different. She and Tony had come to these people's house and asked for help—which meant she owed them the truth.

Hands clenched tightly together, she started with Duvalle's attack.

"It wasn't a random act of violence, was it?" Jessie asked.

Marianne shook her head. "He's a loose cannon—from our past." With a gulp, she started on the background of the Rossi Gang and saw Jessie struggling to keep her expression impassive.

"You were just a kid!" her friend said. "Why is he after you now?"

"On their last bank job, he shot a guard, and my father was wounded. Apparently we all fled to an abandoned house—where my father died in a fire." She wheezed. "We think Duvalle is looking for money that went missing."

"You don't have to tell me any more," Jessie murmured, laying a sympathetic hand on her shoulder.

"No. I want to explain the whole thing." Well, most of it, she thought. Jessica didn't need to hear the bit about how she'd claimed to be Tony's wife. "Before my father died, I was downstairs listening to the men talk. Tony's convinced that Duvalle thinks I know where the money was hidden. But I don't remember anything. I've blocked out that whole part of my life." She raised her eyes to Jessie's. "Tony, my mother, his father, they all thought it was better that way. It wasn't until after Duvalle attacked me that Tony filled me in."

When she finished, she was shaking. Then she saw Miguel standing in the doorway and stopped worrying about her checkered past. "How is Tony?"

"Good. And lucky. The bullet went through muscle tissue and came out the other side. I've given him an antibiotic, so there shouldn't be any infection."

She inhaled the news like a draft of cool, clean air. "Thank you, Miguel. Thank you so much."

"It's the least I can do."

"Can I see him?"

"He won't be too coherent. I've given him something for the pain and something to help him sleep. He'll feel better in the morning."

Crossing quickly to the exam room, she looked around and was startled to find it empty.

Miguel turned and pointed toward a section of paneling that opened into a door. "I have a room in the back. People stay here from time to time when they need shelter."

The statement was simple and unemotional, but Marianne knew that it held a wealth of meaning. Miguel had been on the run himself, and he understood very well what it was like to need a safe place to stay.

"Thank you," Marianne whispered, knowing that if she tried to speak louder, her voice would crack. She had thought she and Tony were alone in this. But help had been closer than she'd suspected.

Miguel stepped aside, and she entered a cheerfully furnished bedroom. Tony's clothes were lying over the arm of a chair, and he was stretched out on a double bed, his arm properly bandaged and the covers pulled to his waist.

His skin was pale, and dark, half-moon circles stood out below his eyes. But he was breathing peacefully, and the bandage on his arm looked clean and white, with no signs of fresh blood.

His eyes flickered open when she came down beside him and clasped his good hand.

"How are you?"

"About to conk out. Sorry," he apologized, his words slurred. His hand tightened ever so slightly on hers, but it was obvious that simply clenching his fingers was a major effort.

"Just sleep. And mend." Leaning over, she brushed her lips against his forehead. "I'll be here if you need anything."

He settled back against the pillows, his face contorting for a moment.

"What?" she asked anxiously. "Are you in pain?"

"Yeah. But it will…go away…" The disjointed words trailed off. She sat beside him, watching him off to sleep, then gently untangled her fingers from his, tensing when he stirred. She didn't want to wake him. He needed rest.

She wanted to keep watch, but thought she should speak to Miguel and Jessie again. So she brushed one last kiss against his cheek and stood.

When she returned to the waiting room, her hosts were quietly talking.

She caught the phrase "bank robbers" and knew they had been discussing the Rossi Gang. "I was filling Miguel in—if that's okay," Jessie said quickly.

"Of course."

"I am honored that you trust us," Miguel said gravely. "You'll need to stay for a few more days while Tony rests and gets his strength back."

"I wouldn't count on his getting much rest," Marianne murmured. "He won't want to sit still, let alone lie down."

"I know what it's like convincing a proud man that he needs someone to look after him," Jessie said, glancing pointedly at her husband, before turning back to Marianne. "I can lend you some clothes," she added. "And we…keep stuff around for visitors. So there's bound to be something that will fit Tony."

"Thank you," Marianne answered, overwhelmed by their kindness and the care they were taking.

"Right now, you need to get off your feet," Miguel said, then hesitated for a moment. "Are you and Tony—" He stopped, then started again. "Do you want to sleep down here with him? Or somewhere else?"

She felt her cheeks go warm, but didn't care how much she gave away by her answer. "Here."

Miguel kept his tone professional. "If he needs any medical attention, there's an intercom beside the bed. And I've left more pain medication on the bedside table." He glanced at his watch. "In four hours, he can have some more if he asks for it."

Marianne nodded, afraid that if she tried to thank them again, she'd burst into tears. When the Valeros left, she tiptoed back to the bedroom. He was sleeping soundly. For several minutes she stood looking at him, seeing the lines of stress on his face—even in sleep. Or maybe they were from the pain.

She wanted to slide down on the bed and gather him to her. But that would serve her own needs, not his. Instead, she slipped into the bathroom for a quick shower before putting on her T-shirt again and easing onto the bed.

As soon as her mind was free from other thoughts, she felt a wave of guilt—and an overwhelming need to tell Tony how Duvalle had found them. Unfortunately, that was going to have to wait.

Chapter Eight

When Marianne awoke and her eyes focused on the painting of a tropical flower garden on the wall across the room, she blinked. Then she turned her head and saw Tony, the bed-covers pulled to his waist and a white bandage on his left arm.

His eyes were open, and she caught a tender and un-guarded expression on his face that made her heart squeeze. Before she could assure herself that it wasn't her imagination, he rearranged his features.

"How are you?" she whispered, wanting to know about the gunshot—and more.

"Okay."

"Good." She touched the back of her hand lightly to the dark stubble on his cheek, stroking the rough surface with her fingers, the way she'd wanted to that first night when he'd come down to the beach house and found her. Then she'd had no right to touch him. Now—now they had made love. And that changed everything—or did it?

For several heartbeats, neither of them moved, except for the gentle motion of her fingers.

"Tony?" she murmured.

He turned his head, his mouth brushing her flesh, and she felt his warmth as well as the erotic nibbling of his lips. It brought back memories of the night before.

She felt her insides go hot and moist as she remembered how it had been with her body rocking against his. Now here they were in bed again.

His eyes locked with hers as his teeth played with the edge of her finger, sending little shock waves of sensation through her.

"Marianne." When he reached for her, he couldn't conceal a wince of pain.

"Your arm hurts." Lord, she was picturing herself making love with him—when he had gotten shot last night because of her.

"I'll live," he answered dismissively.

"You need more pain medication," she said, turning toward the night table where Miguel had left the tablets.

Tony shook his head. "No. I want to keep my head clear so we can have a little discussion."

She didn't like the sound of that last comment, or the expression on his face as he slowly pushed himself to a sitting position and fixed his steely gaze on her in a way that made her chest tighten painfully.

"I told you to climb out the window and meet me at the car," he growled.

She shrugged and scooted up, so that her face was nearly level with his. "I heard shots—and you were in there."

"All the more reason to run the other way!"

"I wasn't just going to leave you in a burning house! You got shot because of me."

His eyes darkened. "I should have known better than to stay at the beach house."

Instantly, a vice seemed to grip her middle. "No! It wasn't your fault."

"Oh?"

The questioning look in his eyes made her gulp. She wanted to turn away, instead, she spoke in a rush. "Tony, Duvalle couldn't have found us at your father's unless he knew to poke around Paradise Beach.'' She gulped then went on. ''I bought gas at a station on the edge of town. I—I wasn't thinking. And I used my credit card.'' She dipped her head. ''I'm sorry.''

He didn't answer for several seconds, then slid his palm up and down her arm. ''You're just guessing that's how he got to the area. He could have researched me and my father up the kazoo.''

''Maybe. But I still made a mistake. Are you're saying it's okay for me to make an error in judgment, but not for you?''

''Right.''

''Why?''

''Because I should know better.''

''You mean because you have to be perfect—the way your father wanted? And I get to be human?''

As she felt the tension zinging back and forth between them, she realized nothing fundamental had changed. He was still dealing with her the way he had since they were kids. He was protecting her, taking responsibility, making decisions. Because his dad had given him that job.

The only thing different was that she'd enticed him into her bed. Now he was probably feeling guilty that he'd let himself be seduced by a virgin.

She was the one who looked away first, because she didn't know what to say. It seemed he didn't either, because the silence stretched like a watch spring wound too tightly.

The impasse was broken by a knock at the door.

The look of relief that flashed across Tony's face made her throat tighten. ''Yes?'' he called out.

The door opened, and Miguel stepped into the room, his expression carefully neutral as he looked toward the bed. ''I was waiting for you to wake up.'' Setting down a small pile of clothing on the dresser, he turned to Marianne. ''Jessie thinks these will fit you.''

"Thank you."

"How are you?" he asked Tony.

"Tolerable. What time is it?"

"Close to noon."

Tony shook his head. "You must have given me enough knockout drops to bring a horse down."

"Not quite. Just enough to make sure you'd get a good night's sleep. Come out to the exam room so I can have a look at the arm."

He strode from the room, and Tony tossed aside the covers. When he looked around for his clothes, Marianne took his pants off the chair and handed them to him.

It was obvious that putting them on hurt his arm, but she was pretty sure he wouldn't want her help getting dressed. So she grabbed the clothing Jessie had sent down and shut herself in the bathroom.

Fifteen minutes later, when she emerged and went into the exam room, she found that Miguel had finished with the bandage on Tony's arm.

Putting down the roll of gauze, the physician cleared his throat as he looked at her. "Last night you told Jessie the man who attacked you, Duvalle, is looking for money from a bank robbery, and he thinks you know where it's hidden. But your problem is that you can't remember any details from that time in your life."

She nodded tightly.

"If the memories are buried in your subconscious, maybe there's a way to bring them to the surface."

"How?" she asked.

"Hypnosis."

Tony's eyes darkened. "Forget it! Messing with her mind could be dangerous."

"No. Wait. I want to hear about it," she objected.

"Abby Franklin, one of the psychologists at 43 Light Street, has used it on a number of my patients," Miguel continued. "Individuals who had traumatic experiences in Latin America and needed to remember pertinent details so that they could apply for political asylum."

"Can you guarantee it's not harmful?" Tony challenged.

"I can't give you an absolute guarantee," Miguel responded quietly. "But I can tell you that Abby will be very careful. Why don't you call her and talk about it?" He held out a business card with the phone number, and Marianne took it, her hand closing tightly around the white rectangle.

"I don't think it's a good idea," Tony muttered.

"Let's at least hear what she has to say," she answered, feeling a swell of hope—and fear. He had wrestled with demons from the past for years. She had locked those demons in a place where they couldn't tear at her. Yet as she'd driven to Baltimore last night, she'd realized she had to know the truth.

Before she lost her nerve, she went to find a phone. By the time she reached the front hall, the card was a mangled mess in her grasp, and she had to smooth it out to read the number.

When she returned to the bedroom, after giving Abby a frank account of her background, Tony wasn't there. She finally found him in the kitchen, wearing a long-sleeved shirt that covered his bandage and stonewashed jeans. He was sipping a cup of black coffee.

"You're through with the phone?" he asked.

"Uh-huh."

"Then I'll call Mike Lancer."

"Tony, you and I have to talk."

"Not now!" With a jerky motion he rose from the table and exited the room, leaving her staring down at the half-full cup of coffee. She could have followed him and forced a confrontation, though she wasn't sure it would do either one of them much good at the moment.

HE STEPPED into the den, being careful not to slam the door behind him—knowing that he was hiding from Marianne and from himself. For long moments he stood staring at the phone, but he couldn't force his mind to focus on calling Mike Lancer.

Marianne wanted to finish the conversation they'd started in bed. No way was he prepared for that.

He grimaced. All of his adult life, he'd understood his goals, worked toward them, and accomplished what he set out to do. Maybe at the beginning he'd been out to prove to his father that he was better than Vance Rossi would ever be. But showing up his dad had slipped way into the background as he'd become his own man.

In the space of two days, however, everything had changed. Arlan Duvalle had thrown his life into chaos. And nothing was under his control anymore.

The worst part was that he'd lost his center of gravity—and he was having trouble finding it again, because it had shifted. He'd thought that he'd made himself self-sufficient. Over the past few days, he'd discovered how much he needed Marianne Leonard in his life. He was still shaken by the revelation—and shaken by the knowledge that he'd almost lost her. When he'd come to and seen her with that burning rug in her arms, he'd almost gone insane.

She'd done it for him. She'd done every damn thing he'd asked her to do, and more—except keep her distance from him.

Now she was going to get herself hypnotized, for God's sake—because he'd forced her to try and remember the night of the fire. And he was scared spitless at the prospect, because there was no way of knowing what it would do to her.

But there could be a way to head her off, he suddenly realized. If Mike Lancer could get a line on Duvalle before the hypnotist arrived, maybe he could persuade her that she didn't need to go ahead with the session.

Feeling a surge of hope, he reached for the phone. Unfortunately, Mike was out of the office. All he could do was leave a message on the answering machine, asking him to call Miguel Valero's as soon as possible.

Putting down the receiver, he slumped in the desk chair. He might have paced the room, waiting for the phone to ring. But he was starting to feel light-headed, so he leaned back and closed his eyes. Minutes later, he was asleep.

MARIANNE DIDN'T SEE Tony again until Abby Franklin arrived and he followed them into the Valeros' comfortable sitting room. Instead of taking a seat, he remained standing, leaned against the door jamb, gazing down at them like a judge about to sentence a couple of criminals.

"This is a bad idea," he growled.

"Maybe it's the only way to find out about the money."

"Forget the money."

She stared at him incredulously. "For two days we've been trying to figure out where the money went. Now you're saying you just want to forget about it?"

"We already know Duvalle isn't going to give up. He'll come after us again. All we have to do is make sure we pick the time and place. So we don't need a damn psychologist poking into your mind."

She moistened her suddenly dry lips. "Is there some reason you're afraid to find out what really happened that night?"

His face turned white, and she could see the question had shaken him to the core. "That's not the point. The point is that *you* look like you're on the way to an execution."

"I'm nervous. I think that's natural."

After several moments' hesitation, he pushed away from the jamb. "Okay, have it your way."

Silence filled the room as he exited and quietly closed the door.

Marianne looked down at her hands, twisting them in her lap. "I apologize for that crack he made about you," she whispered.

"Well, he's very protective of you," Abby answered.

"He's been watching out for me since we were kids," she shot back. "It was an obligation his father put on him."

"I think it's a little more personal than that."

"Right. I'm like his little sister who doesn't have sense enough to come in out of the rain. He's even mad at me for going back into the house when he and Duvalle were fighting it out."

"From where I'm sitting, he's not acting like a big brother. I'd say he's acting more like a man who wants to make sure his woman is protected."

Marianne felt her heart lurch inside her chest. With her training, could Abby see something that wasn't obvious?

"How do you feel about him?" the psychologist asked.

Well, she knew how to answer *that* question. "I've loved him for a long time," she said, astonished that she had blurted out the confession after five minutes with this woman whom she'd only met a few times. She squeezed her eyes shut, then opened them again. "There are a lot of issues between us. Stuff about our fathers—about the way we grew up. I got it in my head that if…if we made love, everything would change. But it hasn't."

"The experience didn't live up to your expectations?" Abby asked quietly.

"It was wonderful," she whispered, feeling her whole body turn warm. "But my guess is that he feels guilty about letting me tempt him. And he sure as heck can't stop playing the role of bodyguard. That's not what I want. I want him to act like we're in this together."

The therapist gave her a reassuring smile. "Well, the two

of you are in a pressure cooker right now. That makes working out your relationship difficult. Don't give up on him until things settle down."

Marianne sat very still, her thoughts turned inward.

"What are you thinking about?" Abby asked.

"I thought he wanted me to remember where the money was hidden, so we could set a trap for Duvalle. Now I'm sort of confused."

"If you want a quick analysis, I'd say he thinks the money is less important than your emotional well-being. And he's afraid that revisiting the day of the fire will be too traumatic for you to handle."

"You think *that's* why he's afraid to let me have this session with you?" she breathed.

"Well, I don't ordinarily make snap judgments. But that's what I think—off the top of my head."

Marianne nodded, trying to wrap her mind around that.

"The question is, what do you want to do?" the therapist asked.

"I want to find out what I've been hiding from myself all these years."

"Good. Because it's important to want this for yourself."

"I do. So maybe we'd better get started," she pressed, praying that she wouldn't lose her nerve.

"Okay. If we had more time, I'd spend several sessions with you before getting into age-regression hypnosis. But this is kind of a special situation. So let me tell you a little about the technique I'd like to try. I use it regularly with people who have lived through disturbing events they can't recall. Really, it's self-hypnosis. And I'm just there to guide you back in time and help you control the experience—so you'll feel more like an observer than a participant." When she'd gone into a bit more detail, she asked, "Do you have any questions?"

"No."

"Then make yourself comfortable," Abby said, pulling her chair closer. "Raise your eyes just a little and look up at the line where the wall meets the ceiling."

She obeyed.

"Now I'm just going to help you relax," Abby continued in a soothing voice. "Where would you like to go on vacation if you had the chance?"

Marianne had had enough of the beach. "The mountains," she answered.

"Good. Then imagine you're in a beautiful mountain forest, sitting next to a rushing stream. You can hear the water tumbling over the rocks, and you can feel the cool wind on your face."

She let the soothing sound of Abby's voice put her into the scene. Soon she felt herself drifting, relaxing, letting go of her anxiety.

"Can you talk to me?" Abby asked.

"Yes," she answered, although it was hard to get the word out.

"Good. Do you want to try going back to your childhood?"

She hesitated for a moment, then whispered, "Yes."

"Okay, imagine you're looking at a big TV screen across the room from you. It's got a calendar on it with this year. Can you see it?

"Yes."

"We'll start by flipping the calendar back to this time last year. Can you see that?"

When she nodded, Abby continued. "Now we'll go back farther, and instead of the calender you'll see *yourself* on the TV."

They stopped for a typical day in college, high school, middle school and her first year in Baltimore. Finally they reached the year of the fire, and she felt herself getting tense.

"You're going to relax more deeply. You're very relaxed.

Very peaceful," Abby reassured her. "On the TV screen you can see the little girl you were eighteen years ago. But it's like watching someone else. And no matter what happens on the screen, it can't hurt you. Duvalle can't hurt you. The fire can't hurt you. Understand?"

"Yes."

"Good. And remember, you can turn off the television any time you want to." She paused. "It's the afternoon of the fire. Where are you?"

"In my room. Mommy is upset. She's throwing things in suitcases. And she's shouting at Uncle Vance."

"Okay, let's come forward to the evening. Where are you now?"

"In an old broken house."

"Who's there?"

"Me and Daddy. Uncle Vance and Doo Valve."

"Duvalle?"

"Yes."

"Where is Tony?"

"His name is Nick. He and Mommy are getting medicine for Daddy." Marianne lifted her hand, stuck the edge of her finger in her mouth, and sucked.

"It will be easier to talk if you take your hand out of your mouth," Abby said gently.

"Big girls don't suck their fingers," she said, echoing her mother's words.

"Right. So where are you now?"

"I'm at the top of the stairs. But I'm scared. I don't want to be up here all by myself. It's dark. And the moon is so big outside the window. I want to come downstairs. But Doo Valve is shouting. Uncle Vance tells him to go take a hike, so he's going away."

"What do you do?"

"I go down to the room with Daddy and Uncle Vance

and peek in the door. Uncle Vance is talking about the money.''

"The money from the robbery?"

"Yes. He says that Doo Valve wants to take it all and run away. So he's hidden it.''

"Where is it?"

"Under Daddy's sleeping bag. Daddy is lying on it. Uncle Vance says Doo Valve won't find it there.''

"What happens now?"

"Uncle Vance has gone to get some food for us. And I go in to see Daddy.'' She caught her breath as she looked at her father's face. "He's glad to see me,'' she said, the thrill of the memory capturing her. "His voice is always soft and nice when he talks to me. But he got hurt. I'm scared he's gonna die,'' she said, the last part choking off in a little sob. Then she started to shake.

"What's wrong?"

"Doo Valve is coming back in. He's angry with Daddy. They're fighting. I hit him, but he's hurting Daddy.'' Her eyes widened. "No. Oh, no!''

"What?"

"Doo Valve kicked the lantern,'' she gasped. "It fell over on the bandages. They're catching fire.''

She cringed. "The floor is catching fire.''

She was there again. With the little girl on the television screen. As her terror grew, she and the little girl merged into one person.

"Marianne, it's all right. Marianne! Wake up.''

She began to scream then, scream in horror as the terrible memory took control. Leaping off the couch, she started to run from the flames that licked at her skirt, her legs.

Chapter Nine

"Marianne! Marianne!"

Tony's voice. She tried to lock on to his voice. Then his arms were around her, holding her, rocking her, telling her that everything was all right. That she was safe.

Her eyes blinked open, and she didn't know where she was.

"Marianne," he said again, bringing her back to the present. She was in Tony's arms. Safe in his arms. Lifting her into his lap, he cradled her trembling body against his.

With all her strength, she clung to him, as she tried to catch her breath.

"What did you do to her?" he demanded, tossing the angry question at Abby like a warrior hurling a spear.

"Don't," Marianne managed. "It's okay." She sucked in a breath and let it out in a rush. "She took me back to the day of the fire. I saw it. I know what happened. I didn't do it!"

His eyes were fierce. "Didn't do what? What are you talking about?"

She gulped. "Oh, Tony, I was afraid I was the one who knocked over the lantern. I thought I started the fire that killed Daddy! That's why I was so afraid to remember that night."

He stared at her, and she knew he was struggling to absorb her confession—and her vast relief.

"But it wasn't me," she sobbed out. "It wasn't me. It was Duvalle! He hit the lantern with his foot when he was fighting with Daddy!"

"And all this time, deep down, you were afraid you had done it?" Abby asked gently.

"Yes!" Tears stung her eyes, tears of relief.

"What you're describing can happen to sensitive children," Abby said gently. "When a parent or a sibling dies, the child thinks she's somehow responsible. In your case, you were afraid to deal with it, so you swept it out of your mind."

Marianne nodded, taking the words in as Tony's arms tightened around her.

"I didn't understand," he muttered. "I thought you were too traumatized by being caught in the fire to remember what happened that night."

"I was. But it was more than that." Raising her head, she looked at Abby. "Thank you for helping me."

"You had a very strong reaction." The psychologist spread her hands apologetically. "I'm sorry. I thought I could help you keep your distance from the experience."

"It was frightening. But it was worth it," she answered. "I saw my father's face," she breathed. "I heard him speak to me. He called me Lil' Bit."

"That was his pet name for you," Tony said softly.

"Yes. And I won't lose the memory of him again," she vowed. "He may have taken a wrong turn in his life, but he wasn't a bad man. He loved me."

"I know," Tony said, his voice thick. "I used to see the way you were together and envy you. My dad could never unbend that much."

She reached for his hand, twining her fingers with his,

longing to share the insights that the experience had given her. "Your father had flaws. But he loved you, too."

"I used to think he had a funny way of showing it."

"He was doing the best he could to take care of you—even if the way he did it was misguided. But the letter he left you says a lot about his character."

"Yeah. It says he didn't want to face me. It says he had to make sure I wasn't around to react."

She wanted to tell him she'd seen the same traits in the son. She knew it wouldn't serve any purpose. "A lot has been happening in the past few days," she said instead. "Too much to take in all at once. I understand, because I'm having the same problem as you."

He nodded.

In the silence that followed, she let her mind drift back over the scene, amazed that she could view it without the terror. "If you still want to hear about it, I found out about the money," she said in a low voice.

Tony's features sharpened, but all he said was "Okay."

"Your father and mine were talking about it—and I heard. It was under Daddy's sleeping bag."

"In the room where the fire started?" he clarified.

"Yes. It must have burned up..." She stopped, then forced herself to finish the sentence. "...with him."

Tony's fingers stroked her. "I'm sorry about your father."

"I know. But I lost him a long time ago." She spread her palms upward. "At least now I know what his face looks like. At least I know he loved me. And I know the fire wasn't my fault. Thank the Lord." She turned toward Tony. Maybe she'd come to terms with the past. But the present was still a mess. "You said you wanted to set a trap for Duvalle. We need to set things up so he thinks he's got *us* trapped."

"The Light Street Irregulars can help you," Abby interjected.

"Who are they?" Tony asked.

"That's the name we've given the group of friends who help each other when one of us is in trouble. Like last year, when Miguel and Jessie were being stalked by a killer."

Tony nodded. "I let Miguel use my house for a while, but I thought the guys from the barrio were hiding him."

"Light Street got involved later," Abby explained. "I can set up a meeting with them. A lot of the men work for Randolph Security now, but they ran covert operations for various government agencies. We don't advertise all this, for obvious reasons." She turned toward Marianne. "If you'd been at the foundation longer, you would have found out about us. I'm just glad we can help you out now."

Abby made a phone call to Randolph Security. When she got off the phone, she looked pleased. "They can meet with you this evening. Seven o'clock. Here."

"Good," Marianne answered, just as Tony's beeper went off. When he checked the number, it turned out the call had been made from his own house.

His face was wary as he used the special equipment that Miguel had had installed to prevent calls from being traced and phoned home. After hearing who was on the other end of the line, he relaxed a notch.

"It's Mike Lancer," he mouthed.

She knew him. He was a private detective who worked with her friend Jo O'Malley.

She could tell Mike was talking rapidly, and that Tony didn't like what he was hearing.

"What is it?" she asked.

He waved her to silence and gripped the receiver. "When?" he asked. Then, "I'll meet you there!"

Mike must have objected to the plan, because Tony came

back with a sharp insistence. When he hung up, his face was grim.

"What happened?" Marianne asked.

"I asked Mike to check up on Duvalle. He stopped by my house and found the place had been searched."

"I take it you want to go over there—and he wants you to stay put."

"He doesn't know what to look for. I'm the only one who can tell if anything important is missing."

When he started for the door, she raised her voice a notch. "You can't go over there."

"Why the hell not?"

"It could be a trap. Duvalle could *want* you to come. He could—"

He cut her off in mid-sentence. "In the first place, Mike says Duvalle is long gone."

"How does he know?"

"I left the air-conditioning on. The back door was open long enough for the heat to build up. Mike didn't find anyone inside. Probably Duvalle searched the place before he came to Paradise Beach."

The clipped sentences brooked no argument, but she mounted one, anyway. "I hope you're not thinking about driving yourself."

Tony moved his arm, concealing a grimace. "I'll be fine."

"Shall we ask your doctor?"

When he scowled, she relented. "If you insist on going, I can drive you."

"I don't want you out of this house until we know Duvalle is in custody."

"Why is it different for me than for you?"

"Mike and I can take care of ourselves," he snapped.

"I know you can. But you're not exactly in top shape.

You were wounded last night." As soon as she said it, she immediately regretted reminding him.

For several seconds he stared at her stonily, then sighed. "All right, you can haul me around!"

When he stalked into the hall, Marianne turned apologetically to Abby. "Sorry."

"It's okay. He's dealing with a lot of problems—and trying to figure out how to do the right thing by you."

"Exactly. Protect me."

Abby gave her a reassuring smile. "Trust me, it's more than that."

Praying it was true, Marianne joined Tony in the hall. He looked gray and fatigued, and she was certain that going over to his house was the wrong thing to do. For a nanosecond it flitted through her mind that she should simply tell him they were going to stay put and let Mike Lancer take care of any immediate problems. Instead she went to ask Jessie if she could borrow her car, which would be less recognizable than his.

Ten minutes later, they were on their way.

"I'm sorry I snapped at you," he apologized.

"It's okay. I know you're under a lot of pressure. We both are." She waited, hoping that might get them into a conversation, but he chose to pass up the opportunity.

When they reached his street of large brick two-story homes, Tony sat up straighter. "Drive around the block, I want to make sure our friend isn't lying in wait,"

She made a slow circuit of the streets as they both scanned the scene. When he was satisfied that the house wasn't under surveillance, he asked her to park in back of his next door neighbor's garage.

As soon as Tony stepped through the kitchen door, he made a low sound that was part anger, part surprise. "I guess Mike didn't want to give me the bad news," he muttered as he surveyed his well-appointed kitchen. The polished maple cabinets stood open and broken glasses, bowls and china were strewn across the granite countertops and the Italian tile floor.

Marianne drew in a sharp breath. "Oh Lord, what a mess."

"I've got a cleaning service. They can take care of it," he said with amazing calm as he guided her around the worst of the mess. Still, their shoes crunched on broken glass that ground itself into the surface of the expensive tile, and she knew it was going to take more than a cleaning service to set things to rights. Obviously Duvalle had taken out his frustration on the house. Hopefully, that meant he hadn't found anything important.

"Mike?" Tony called as he strode down the hall.

"Be with you in a minute," the detective called from upstairs.

Marianne drew in a breath, stiffening as she picked up Duvalle's scent.

"He was here. I can smell him," she whispered.

"Yeah."

The conversation came to an abrupt halt as the sound of running water reached them.

"What the hell?" Yanking open a door, Tony flipped on a light and peered down a flight of steps leading to what she knew was a plush recreation room and an office complex.

An oath tumbled from his lips as he switched on the lights and started down.

Marianne squinted over his shoulder and saw that the floor of the recreation room was covered with water.

"Either the bastard opened a valve, or he punched a hole in the water heater. No wonder Mike wouldn't tell me about it over the phone," Tony ground out. "The whole house is going to smell like mold before this dries."

"A pump and a couple of fans will work wonders," she said, hoping it was as simple as that.

"I hope." He looked around again and bellowed, "Mike!"

"In a minute," the detective called to them.

"Thanks for filling me in," Tony muttered under his breath as they sloshed their way to the office where modern equipment was juxtaposed with expensive antique pieces.

He squished across the oriental rug to several cardboard boxes on the floor that held letters and other papers. After shuffling through them, he opened a large antique armoire where more boxes were neatly stacked on shelves. After examining the contents, he let out a breath. "I'm glad I didn't leave any important business stuff on the floor."

"Good."

He stayed facing the shelves, his hands pressed to his sides.

Quietly she moved up behind him, aware that she had him cornered. The only way out of the room was around her—or through her. "Tony, before Mike gets down here, I want to talk," she said, knowing that there was hardly any chance of starting and finishing a discussion. But anything would be better than the tension she was feeling.

"About what?" he asked, still facing the shelves.

"About how we're going to be with each other from now on. Please don't shut me out."

He faced her.

She stood her ground, unwilling to back down now that she'd gotten his attention. "Are you feeling like I piled another obligation on you? Or are you just wishing things would go back to the way they used to be?"

"They can't go back. I've pushed you to remember stuff that you locked away. I've changed the whole structure of your life."

"Oh, Lord, Tony, is that what you think? It wasn't you

who did it. It was Duvalle. And…and even though it was hard to face the truth, I'm better for it. Don't you know that? Don't you know that what I need now is some honest communication with you? I want to know how you feel about us.''

He made a low sound in his throat as he reached for her, hauling her to him as his mouth came down on hers. Startled, she gasped, and he took shameless advantage of her open lips—swamping her with a kiss that demanded surrender or flight.

Her only real choice was surrender, heart and soul, mind and body. She returned the kiss with a fierceness that seemed to stun him, then fuel his ardor.

When he finally lifted his mouth, her head was spinning.

''Do you have any better idea of how I feel?'' he growled.

''I think so.''

''Good.'' He looked around the office, then pulled her to the far side of the armoire, blocking them from view. With a deep groan of satisfaction, he drew her body tightly to his. She came willingly, unable to fight the need to be as close as possible.

Leaning his back against the paneled wall, he splayed out his legs and brought her between them, his good hand sliding over her hips and wedging her firmly against his erection.

He kissed her again, his lips lazy and warm, while his good hand began to do very provocative things to her breasts—things that would drive her over the edge if he kept them up.

''Tony. You shouldn't be doing this,'' she gasped, her knees so weak that she slumped forward against him. ''Not until you're better.''

''Well—maybe not standing up,'' he answered, his stroking fingers shifting to her back, drawing tiny circles. In her present state, the caress was only slightly less erotic.

"Do you know what it would have done to me if Duvalle had hurt you again?" he asked softly.

"Yes. The same thing it would have done to me if something had happened to you. It's no different."

He gathered her closer, and she listened to the ragged edge of his breathing and her own, her mind drifting.

Yet as she sucked in breath, an unpleasant scent wafted toward her, stronger, more immediate than a few minutes ago.

"What's wrong?"

"He's here!" she hissed, dread grabbing her even as she tried to tell herself it wasn't true.

"Mike. Yeah, we'd better cut this out before Mike catches us."

"Not Mike."

Whirling to the desk, she picked up the phone receiver. There was no dial tone. Frantically she pressed repeatedly at the button—with the same results.

"It's dead," she whispered, feeling the skin crawl on the back of her neck. "He took care of Mike. We're next."

"We've got to get out of here!" Tony climbed onto the desk, grabbed her hand, and reached to work the catch on the window high up in the wall. The mechanism wouldn't slide.

From the hall, she heard the sound of water sloshing, then an eerily familiar voice in the hallway. "If you're trying to open the window, don't bother. I nailed it shut from the outside. You're trapped. The way you were always trapped."

Marianne and Tony both froze—reacting to the voice as much as to the cruel observation. It sounded like Silvio Marco speaking. Only it couldn't be Silvio Marco. He was dead.

Tony's face had gone white, his body taut. "Dad?" he

gasped, starting to move away from the protection of the partition.

Marianne grabbed his arm and squeezed. "No."

"Look's like you're not free of me yet, kid" the mocking voice continued.

"That's not your father," Marianne whispered urgently. "It's Duvalle. He did this before—used your father's voice when he attacked me."

Tony blinked and straightened. Taking hold of Marianne's shoulders, he thrust her back so that she was behind him, and a protruding section of wall shielded them both from the door.

"What about Mike?" she whispered. "How can we get him downstairs?" *If he's still alive,* she thought.

Duvalle must have been straining to hear them, because he laughed again. "If you're waiting for your P.I. friend to rescue you, you're out of luck. It wasn't him who called you on the phone half an hour ago. It was me—pretending to be him."

"What?" Marianne breathed.

"Don't you get it yet?" their tormentor continued. "Lancer isn't here. He's off on a wild-goose chase to the Marco warehouse. It wasn't hard to figure out your boyfriend was working with him, once I got a line on your phone records from Paradise Beach."

Tony uttered a curse.

"How…how did you find us at the beach house?" Marianne stammered.

"Your credit card at the gas station. Then some old geezer in the local bar was bragging about seeing you."

When she made a low sound, Tony reached back and stroked her shoulder. "It's okay," he murmured.

Duvalle began to speak again. "If you're wondering how I learned his voice, all I had to do was listen to his answering-machine message a couple of dozen times. I can do